A Single Moment in Time

BERNADETTE ZAWISTOWSKI

authorHOUSE®

AuthorHouse™
1663 Liberty Drive
Bloomington, IN 47403
www.authorhouse.com
Phone: 1 (800) 839-8640

This is a work of fiction. All of the characters, names, incidents, organizations, and dialogue
in this novel are either the products of the author's imagination or are used fictitiously.

Published by AuthorHouse   09/06/2016

ISBN: 978-1-5246-3813-9 (sc)
ISBN: 978-1-5246-3812-2 (e)

Library of Congress Control Number: 2016914640

Print information available on the last page.

Any people depicted in stock imagery provided by Thinkstock are models,
and such images are being used for illustrative purposes only.
Certain stock imagery © Thinkstock.

This book is printed on acid-free paper.

CHAPTER 1

SHE CURSED A THIRD TIME at the little man from the car rental place, her little white car did not make it from the west to east of Ireland it just went 30 miles east from his business. Thanking her lucky stars, it was just two miles from the heart of a town. By Ireland standards but in America it was a street that her car started to slowly die. Anne could still hear that little man says, 'Oh my dear, if this car could float it would take herself back to the America.'

Anne can only imagine what could make the car sound like it's a dying animal and the smoke.

Anne coast into a driveway, she looks at the cottage and smiles; thinking to herself, 'God how I missed this place.' she leaves a note on the car and on the 'wee' cottage door. Anne heads to the center of town and smiles. 'It even smells the same.'

There was a chill in the air and a dampness that didn't bother Anne. When she was back in the states she would try to recall that feeling she would get when she was here in Ireland but all it got she was a pair of ruined sneakers and a cold.

Anne knew this walk so well; she could do it in her sleep. The dips of each worn hill, the small stones and large potholes.

Anne smiled. It was nice to see that not many things have changed. Anne pulled up on her camera bag, brushing her curly brown hair from her face as the wind blew at her.

As she came to the town she knew and loved, taking a deep breath she wondered, 'Would they remember me, it has been twelve years, would himself or did he get married?' Anne smiled, 'You already have the talk.'

She shakes her head and continuing toured the town.

'Oh Benhern' This sleepy town was just as beautiful as she remembered it. She walked every inch of this town in addition, met the people she had grown to love like her own family. She came to this town to trace her family history but what she found instead was a love that nearly killed her and a way with the pictures that would tell a story with just a snap of her camera. The pictures grew into a large bank account though the man didn't grow into anything but heart ache.

'What were you thinking Anne, the man who could have easily been a Hollywood movie star with that built, those eyes that could look right into your soul and, when he spoke . . . 'Oh it was toe curling.' 'Well at least my love of the picture didn't fall about like our marriage Mr. O'Rourke.' Anne spoke to herself.

It was only 8:30 at night and the town looked like everyone was in bed for the night, but Anne knew better.

She will have to call to get the car towed and find a B and B. Anne wasn't a big fan for those. The idea of sharing a bathroom, eating with strangers, it was as if she was staying at a person's home who doesn't speak English and trying to make each other comfortable. Taking a deep breath she pushed on hoping that this visit will be short, sweet and painless.

Just round the corner there was this small pub called O'Flynn's. This small pub was painted yellow and red. For some strange reason the owner couldn't make up his mind or he was having a fight with his wife, Anne never found out. Inside the pub Anne can remember the sights and smells.

That beautiful hand carved bar. That long bar was the center of the pub and the corner tables that would surround the bar and a couple of around table that only the young people would sit.

At the bar there would be Michael who owned and ran the bar, with the grand laugh you ever heard and the most wonderful man with the biggest heart. She wonders if her pictures are still hung on the wall behind the bar.

She wasn't sure if anything she knew would be here. As she came upon a small yellow building she remembers as the best candy and bread shop in the world. Anne would buy bread by the loafs, she remembers a red bike that would lean up against the building every day. When you saw the red bike you know that Betsy the little old lady would make everything in that shop and her six boys and one girl who became one of Anne's closest friend.

'Holy Lord seven kids!', that thought just made Anne shake her head and wonder how Betsy did it on her own. Her husband died from the cancer. God Bless Betsy.

Anne looked at the yellow building and notices that the bike wasn't there. She approached the yellow building and looked in the window.

Anne saw that inside everything was the same but where was the red bike? Betsy and her family lived on the second floor of her shop. "Well a lot can happen a lot in twelve years."

Just then an elderly couple came the small incline.

Anne smiles not looking at the couple and says with a smile in her voice, "Excuse me could you tell me if Betsy still own this shop?"

"Oh my dear Betsy passed about 8 years ago," the old man smiled. "Her daughter, Sammy took over the place, Anne".

Anne took a longer look towards the older couple and smiles, "Uncle Thomas and Aunt Tara!" With a tear in her eyes Anne hugged them both. "Yes it's us my dear." Uncle Thomas said with a smile. As Anne pulled away,

Aunt Tara said. "So my dear what brings you back home?" Aunt Tara has said when Anne left, 'No matter where life brings you, remember this will always be home.'

Anne looked down at her shoes and took a deep breath, "I'm putting a book together with some of the pictures I did in the past. I thought I'd go back."

Aunt Tara smiles, "Oh you're going back." She looks at Uncle Thomas.

He just shook his head, "Now Tara you know better."

Aunt Tara smiles, "Oh Thomas please, you know he hasn't been the same."

Thomas stopped her right there, "Tara, this is none of your concern, he said he's fine and loves his work. Just because you think it's something else and your match making didn't work, just let it go."

Anne looked at them questionably. "Look you two, I just wanted to know if Betsy was still open or not and then I was going to the pub."

Aunt Tara smiled, "Thomas is going after he walks me home."

Anne said, "Well you two, why don't you go home and I'll meet Uncle Thomas at the pub. Oh, the white car in your driveway is mine, it broke down. Damn that little man at the rental shop."

Uncle Thomas smiled as he pulled Aunt Tara. It looks like she was going to say something but Thomas stopped her, "That will be fine dear, save me a seat will you now."

As Anne walked away, out of ear shot Tara said, "Why didn't you let me tell her that Devlin might be there, and if he sees her maybe."

Thomas stopped her and said, "Oh my dear, Devlin is there and if Anne knows he's there she wouldn't go near the pub."

Aunt Tara smiled and said, "I knew I married you for a reason."

He smiled with a twinkle in his eyes.

Tara's smile turns to a frown, "Darling you know getting those two together is like a perfect storm."

Thomas smiles and pats her hand, "Isn't that what they called us?"

CHAPTER 2

ANNE MADE IT TO THE O' Flynn's pub. Anne loved that half the town had her last name but there was no relation to her. Anne climbs the stairs down towards the music and laughter.

As Anne walked toward the bar, the noise level quietly is getting softer and when she reached the bar, she notices that all the air and sound had left the pub. She smiled at the bartender, as she sits. "I'll take two pints of the dark."

The bartender smiled, in her mind she smiled and said back, "Yes Mike, it's me."

At the end of the bar there was a girl and a couple of guys. Anne could feel the eyes burning holes in her direction. The sounds and air was back as Mike gave her the beers and said, "Is himself going to meet you here?"

Anne smiled, "Yes, and thank you."

As Anne lifted the pint of beer she hears the bleach blonde girl at the end of the bartered, "You know Mike, I really don't like those pictures," she points to the pictures Mike proudly displays that Anne took all those years ago. Mike turns to look at the pictures, smiles and then looks at Anne, who just drank her beer but Mike knew she was listening to every word that came out of Sarah's jealous mouth.

"Great. My little sister can do a better job." Sarah finished her beer and looked at Anne.

The pub went silent, everyone waited. Mike just shook his head, "Oh Sarah."

Anne looked up from pictures and winked at Mike.

She stood up and slowly walked towards the end of the bar with her beer in her hand.

Anne and Sarah had always had this hate—hate relationship. You see, Sarah and Anne both loved the same man. But when Devlin and Anne married, the dislike Sarah and Anne shared turned into hate.

As Anne reached the end of the bar, the two boys that were sitting next to Sarah quietly got up, grabbed their pints, and walked out of Anne's way. Placing her beer next to Sarah, Anne takes Sarah's beer.

Standing behind her, Mike tried to make an excuse for Sarah, "Anne, darling herself didn't mean anything by that."

Sarah turns around and faces Anne, with a look that says, "What are you going to do about it?"

Anne smiles, "Just like I mean nothing by this." Anne takes Sarah's beer and dumps the whole glass on to Sarah's head. Anne steps back, as everyone laughs when Sarah jumps off the stool, her green shirt and jeans dripping wet from the beer.

Anne stands and looks at Sarah who is speechless.

Anne looks directly into Sarah's eyes and said, "Sarah, the next time you have something to say about me, you say it to my face."

Anne walks back to her stool as Sarah leaves as fast as her wet jeans can take her.

Anne looks up at Mike and with a smile on her face, "What? I thought I handled myself pretty good."

Mike just shook his head as he turns to serve to the other side of the bar.

Just then Anne knew, right then and there, that he was standing behind her.

"I see that you still have a temper.", Devlin O'Rourke. The man stood 6'4", broad shoulders, jet black hair and ice blue eyes. His voice was deep and that Irish brogue that could make Anne's toe curly and they still do but she wouldn't let him know that.

Anne turned and stood, she was tall but her 5'9" frame 5'11" in her cowboy boots, she felt small compare to Devlin. The pub was quiet and everyone was like waiting for something to happen. 'What would happen, what would they want me to say or do?', Anne thought.

Then from the dark corner Uncle Thomas spoke up, "Well, for the love of Pete, are you two going to kiss or start throwing something?"

Anne looked down at her boots and took a deep breath. She smiled at Devlin and turned to Uncle Thomas, "Your pint is here. I think I've had enough for the night."

Anne was headed for the door but Devlin took a hold of her arm, "Where are you staying?"

Anne was surprised by the question. She looked down at his hand, pulled away, and looked up. She made the mistake looking into his eyes. 'Oh lord. Girl just look away, don't look. Just look away.'

Anne pulled away, "You really have no reason to ask that question, it's no concern to you."

She then realized she had no place to stay, the cottage she once owned, she once owned with Devlin, was sold when she left. Anne never thought she would have any use for the cottage let alone be back in this town and talking to Devlin.

Uncle Thomas spoke up, "She is staying with myself and Tara." Turning to Anne, "In fact your old room is already when ever you're ready to leave."

Anne smiles. "Well then. Mike we'll have another round as I remember we don't leave until someone falls off their bar stool."

Mike smiles, Uncle Thomas raises his empty pint glass and turns to Anne and asked, "You aren't going to spill anyone else pint, are you?" Anne smiles, she could feel Devlin watching her every move, at his table in the coroner of the bar. He could see everything and everyone in the pub. Anne didn't have to look to see Devlin watching her, she could feel his eyes on her.

CHAPTER 3

AS EACH HOUR PASSED, ANNE and Uncle Thomas fell into their old routine. Their talks, their laughers, tears, and so many hugs. It got to the point during the night Anne and Uncle Thomas would drink to all the people in the village, the people who got married, the ones we were going to get married, the children she missed that were born from the past twelve years and the ones who were lost to them. They even drink to the gentleman at the end of the bar who sneezed.

Around 2am Devlin thought to himself 'How can she keeps up with Thomas. Devlin, remembers it only took 2 dark beers and in Anne words, 'I can't feel my teeth, my gums are numb', that memory made Devlin smile, as more memories flooded Devlin mind. The laughter at the bar interrupt his thought.

Seeing Anne laughing at one of Mike's stories.

Uncle Thomas turned around with a wink and a nod.

Devlin nodded in response, he quietly left the bar, knowing she will be fine.

"You, don't have to worry tonight", was the wink from Uncle Thomas. But a thought made him stop in his tracks, 'Who is going to watch Uncle Thomas?'

A Single Moment in Time

Anne slammed her countless pint after losing a bet.

Uncle Thomas was sound asleep, his head on the bar and Mike shook his head at the sight, "All right my dear, it's 3 am, and you need to take himself to his wee cottage."

Anne smiled, "Right you are me, Mike." Ann slowly wiggled off the bar stool, with a little help from the stable bar and went past out Uncle Thomas.

Mike quickly walked around the bar to help both Anne and Uncle Thomas.

Anne with a little slur in her speech, whispered in Uncle Thomas' ear, "Wakie wakie me man."

Mike smiles, places his hand on Thomas shoulder, "Thomas you need to go home before herself wakes up."

With that said, Uncle Thomas wakes up, "Right you are Michael."

Anne smiles, 'Just think, after all these years, Uncle Thomas still doesn't want Aunt Tara to wake up without him.'

Uncle Thomas climbed off his seat more graceful than Anne, but not any better.

So there they were, two oh so quite drunks trying to find their way home. All of a sudden Anne realizes that they had pasted the same bench for the third time.

Anne stopped in mid step. "Hold it Uncle Thomas." Her hand in the air.

He stops and turns to sit down on the bench, "Yes, my dear this is the third time."

Anne laughs and sits next to him.

11

Just then Devlin finds the two cutest couple on the bench just two blocks from the pub. Thankfully Mike called him to let him know that both Thomas and Anne are so drunk that they can't make it off Main Street without circling that 'damn bench'. Devlin walks up to the bench, Anne looks up as Devlin reach them both.

"Oh my, Uncle Thomas,' she pats his knee. "My Dev is here to bring us home."

Devlin felt like someone just kicked him in his stomach.

Uncle Thomas looked up and smiles. "Hello lad, what brings you out on a night like this?"

"Well Thomas, Mike called, I see you two are having trouble.'

Uncle Thomas nods, "Well you know, herself can handle the drink better than she did before."

Anne was on her feet walking towards Uncle Thomas' cottage.

"Oh no Devlin, she's loose.'

Devlin smiles, "Come on." He helps Uncle Thomas up.

"I'm fine, it just I can't handle herself my boy, just help her before she gets hurt."

Uncle Thomas is right. Anne could get hurt in her condition, Devlin thought as he caught up to her.

"So how are the tricks?" Anne asked Devlin looking straight ahead.

Devlin turns to her, "Tricks?

Anne stops, "Yes, you know, how are you? How are things, how is everything?"

Devlin looks at her, "Are you asking me if I'm seeing anyone, dating or married?"

Anne laughs, "My God, you're still are a self-centered bastard! I was just being polite, I don't care if you're seeing anyone, dating or.." Anne swallows a lump that weren't down her throat, "married."

Devlin did notice her hesitation, he smiled.

Anne saw that he smiled, she rolled her eyes and started to walk faster. 'I just need to get to the cottage.'

Devlin caught up to her, "Oh O'Hara, calm down, I was only kidding."

Anne stopped so fast and turns to face him that Devlin slammed right into her, so hard that she was going to fall back but Devlin grabbed her arms. They were so close that Anne noticed that Devlin needed a shave.

'Don't look up, Anne, don't look up.' No matter how much she was yelling at herself, Anne did. She looked up, looked in to his eyes.

"Devlin, I will never be O'Hara again, that person you killed, when you told me the worst thing you ever did was marry me."

Devlin felt like he was slapped in the face.

Anne felt his hold tighten, "Anne, O'Hara is still here. She never left, she was always here. When Mike put your pictures on the wall of his pub, when Tara and Thomas wore that god awful shirt you bought them for their wedding anniversary."

Anne thought, 'I can't do this, I can't.' Anne yelled, "Devlin she is dead!"

Breaking away from him, Anne turns and walks from a stun Devlin.

Uncle Thomas was behind Devlin, watching Anne walk down toward Uncle Thomas and Aunt Tara's cottage.

"You haven't lost her yet, my boy. I don't think you ever did."

CHAPTER 4

ANNE WOKE UP STILL WEARING the same clothes from last night. Anne carefully rolled over on to her back, placed her arm across her eyes. "Oh my God." Even the sound of her own voice made her head hurt. She moaned as she heard a music coming from the kitchen. 'If my head and face didn't hurt I would smile.'

Anne carefully sat up and took a deep breath.

She walked as softly as she could out the door down the hall. One hand holding her stomach, the other holding her head.

The music got louder and her head was pounding more and more.

Aunt Tara was leaning up against the kitchen sink drinking coffee, when Anne made it in to the kitchen.

Aunt Tara shook her head and motion Anne to sit down.

Anne gave her best smile she could and sat down.

Aunt Tara pour Anne a cup of coffee and quietly set it by her and sat down.

Anne took a sip and lean back in the chair, "Oh, I've missed your coffee."

Aunt Tara smiles, "So my dear is it the coffee or was the pub you missed?"

Anne, looked up from her coffee cup, "Oh Tara, you know better than anyone, why I left. He may never know."

Tara smiles and patted her hand, "There my love, you seem to have your mind make up and I know that if I couldn't change your mind then, I guess I can't change it know."

Anne looked questionable across her coffee cup.

"You better behave my dear or I'll leave early than I thought."

"Well," Anne noticed that her head was feeling better after she finished her coffee, "Aunt Tara, I don't know what you put in your coffee but I feel great." Anne said as she placed the cup in the sink.

Looking out the window Anne sees Uncle Thomas in the rose garden. "How does he do it? He drank almost as much I as did and he is out there in the sun, gardening?"

Aunt Tara smiles, "It's magic." as she left the kitchen to go outside to join Uncle Thomas.

Anne looks at the back door as it closes, "I wish I know some magic."

CHAPTER 5

DEVLIN WAS IN HIS KITCHEN sitting with his morning coffee. He's questioning his feeling and thoughts that kept him up all night. 'Why is she back?' 'What has she been doing all these years and is she married, has she a man in her life, or maybe she's not married?'

He clutched his fist, and slammed his hand on the table as he stood up, "Damn you, NOT again."

Devlin got his jacket and stormed out the house, direction unknown.

He just needed to get out. Maybe go for a walk, go check to see if Mr. Donald's completed the future he ordered.

Devlin didn't want to think. 'Just keep busy don't think about her.'

He went through the events that happened last night. Seeing her come down those stairs, just like he wished she would every night after she left.

The hair on the back of his neck stood up even before he saw her. His heart stopped as she walked to the bar unaware he was there and watched every movement she made. He smiled when she encounters Sarah. He remembered what happened when he told Sarah that he was in love with Anne and wanted to marry her. At first Sarah was going to argue with him, but she just smiled and told Devlin he hoped for his sake he made the right choice.

Sarah had known Devlin for a very long time and she knew that if she told him how she felt or spoke ill of Anne, she would lose their friendship as well. After giving him a hug and a smile, Sarah and Devlin knew their life would never be the same again. Little did they know though how their greatly their lives would change.

CHAPTER 6

THE SUN WAS DIRECTLY UP above the trees. Anne smiled at herself, thanking her lucky stars she found her sunglasses. 'It's crazy to think that you could be walking down the road as you turn around the bend and then wham there is a ruined of a castle.'

Anne places her camera bag on the ground. As she adjusted her lens, she stands the starts taking random pictures. Then all of a sudden a wild horse runs from the side of the castle, what would have been the left side of the wall. Anne smiles. 'I wonder what kind of people lived here. Were they were happy? Did they have families? What were their children like?' Anne's thoughts were just running through her mind as she was taking her pictures, getting lost in the view and herself.

Anne stops and smiles. She looks at her digital camera and wonders how she still misses that small canon power shot when she has this wonderful top of the line camera. Was it the great pictures the first time Anne found the small towns, meeting these wonderful people for the first time? How innocent and how happy things were back then.

It's unbelievable to think how much things have changed in a span of twelve years and how things will never be the same again. And no matter how much times has gone by, nothing has or ever will change. Anne placed her camera back in her bag and headed off to another location.

CHAPTER 7

AS ANNE TURNS TO WALK back to the cottage, who does she see coming to her but Father Frances and his fishing pole. Anne smiles as they reach each other.

Father Frances was the town's priest. He married her and Devlin. Father Frances opened his arms and Anne walked into his arms for one of the best bear hugs that she can remember.

Father Frances, "Oh my Anne, how are you doing?"

Anne pulls away to see the smile on his face. 'Oh I tell you, you can't sneeze in this town without everyone knowing.' Anne smiles, "We only circled the bench three times before I noticed."

Father Frances was laughing, "Thomas knew where you two were, he was having his own fun."

Anne shoved Father Frances away from her, "Oh that little man." She laughs. "So where are you heading?"

Father Frances smile faded, "I wanted to go fishing but Thomas was in his rose garden and I didn't want to interrupt."

Anne shook her head, "Oh now come with me." Anne takes his hand and pulls in the direction of the cottage. "You want to play with Thomas, then you will play with Thomas."

Father Frances smiles. Anne looks at him and stops.

"Wait a minute, Uncle Thomas was in his garden and you can't go fishing with him. Did you two cause trouble again and the garden in his punishment?"

Father Frances looked down.

Anne shook her head and smiles, "Well I think Aunt Tara will let him play if I ask for you."

Anne remembers sitting in the pub and watching Father France bless his meal. That wasn't what caught her attention though. It was that everyone was eating meat on Friday. Then Michael leaned over the bar and said, "Listen, you can hear how."

Anne did and this is what she heard, "Once you were cow and pork," as his hand blessed his meal, "Now you are fish."

Anne smiled and shook her head.

Father Frances looks up and whispers, "Oh Thank you my dear. I've been itching to fish with Thomas, I just can't remember where we put our tackle box."

Anne laughs as they head toward the cottage.

Anne had heard the story of Uncle Thomas and Father Frances childhood antics about two weeks after she met them both when they were hiding from Aunt Tara. Anne was at the pub just finishing her lunch when she notices the boys the same time as Aunt Tara called them in as they were walking from the lake after fishing.

They slowly came down the stairs and entered the pub with their heads low and Aunt Tara following behind them. She points at the table in the corner, Uncle Thomas and Father Frances walk to the table and sat down.

Aunt Tara looks at Mike. He smiles but sees that Tara isn't in a good mood. She walks slowly to the bar. Mike nods and comes from behind the bar and sits next to her.

Aunt Tara looks at Mike and says, "Now Michael, what have I told you about those two?"

Mike turns to see both the boys looking down at the table. Mike nods and says, "I know Tara, but they said you were fine, that they didn't need to be grounded."

Tara turns to the table, "So not only did you lie to me but to Michael?"

Uncle Thomas spoke up, "Darling, you said you didn't care what I did, just don't be late for church on Sunday. Well I wasn't late. I was with Frank and we weren't late, just not on time."

Father Frances smiles, "Yes Tara. We were just a little late."

Tara was not buying it, "You of all people, for heaven, sake. You're a priest! You are a man of God. Maybe I was wrong to think you could change."

Uncle Thomas looks at Aunt Tara, "Oh my dear, you know new Frances was chosen by God and he is a good man, but we can't help when the fish are calling us."

"Frances sometimes I really don't know, after this last stunt you two have done. Mike you can go back to the bar."

Tara stands up and walks past the table where Uncle Thomas and Father Frances are sitting, she looks at them and looks at the door, "I just don't know why."

They look at her as she walks out the door.

Uncle Thomas was surprised to see her just leave without telling them what she wants them to do. Just leaving leave like that makes Thomas worry.

Father Frances spoke up and says, "Oh, I think herself maybe she has given up on us."

CHAPTER 8

ANNE LOOKS AT MIKE AND said, "What was that all about?"

Mike smiles, "Thomas and Frances have been childhood friends all their lives. When they were in their teens, both thought they loved the same woman."

Anne was shocked, "Aunt Tara?!?"

Michael smiles, "I know it's hard for you young people to think that we had a life and romance before you."

Anne smiles as she leans closer to Mike, "So tell me the story."

Mike smiles, "Well you see, Tara was always watching out for those two, making sure they didn't get in too much trouble. Tara always knew where they were and if they were ok. Thomas once was fishing and fell in the lake. Frances was on the other side. When Frances saw that Thomas wasn't at the bank of the river he got scared. I think the boys were about 12 or 13 at the time. Frances dropped his pole and started to race around the lake.

Then he saw Tara, she was pulling Thomas out of the lake. Frances said all he could do was watch.

Tara comforted Thomas. When Thomas stood up, she just smiled and walked back to town. I think she was 10 when that happened."

Anne just sat there, she couldn't be thinking, what if that happed to one of her kids? Was there a special bond, or was it just Tara and Ireland?

"Well, after a while if anyone needed to know where the boys were, they just ask Tara." he smiles.

"Then four years later the boys began to notice Tara more and more. One day, after Tara had a run in with a boy from outside the county, Thomas and Frances became her guardian."

Mike looks at the end of the bar where an old man needed a refill. "I'll be right back." As Mike walk behind the bar, "Do you need?" Mike didn't need to finish the questions. He knew the look Anne gave him. She wasn't going anywhere until she heard the whole story.

Anne looks behind her to see Uncle Thomas and Father Frances getting up to leave. They look at Anne and give her a smile. She returns the smile as they leave the pub.

Mike comes back with another pint and sits next to her. "Now where was I? Oh yes. Now the boys are looking after Tara. As they got older it gets a little messy. Tara was becoming the beauty we know now. The boys were taking notice. Tara was never going to come between the boys. She would never play favorite. It was the boys who were having a hard time with deciding who was going to court Tara."

Anne looks at Mike and says, "You mean Tara knew she was going to be with Uncle Thomas?"

Mike smiles, "Yes, but his mother had other plans for him. You see, his mother wanted him to be a priest. Father Frances was going to marry Tara."

Anne smiles, "God does have a strange sense of humor. Uncle Thomas needs Tara. I don't think God could handle Uncle Thomas by himself."

Mike laughs, "You got that right my dear. When Frances and Tara were dating she would ask Frances about the church. His face would light up about the stories and there was passion in his voice. Tara told him that he knows that it's himself God she was talking to, not Thomas. When the three of them got together to tell Thomas's mother that it was Frances that is for the clothe, not Thomas. Tara was going to be Thomas wife. Thomas's mother was not having of any of it, she didn't want to hear it. Then when Frances took Thomas' mother hand and look in to her eyes, Tara told me that Thomas mother saw God's love in Frances eyes and she knew that she couldn't make Frances not follow God, and not give Thomas and Tara a chance of love."

Anne can picture this. She never met Uncle Thomas's mother but she did see a picture. From what Aunt Tara would say, Anne can only imagine what was said.

Picturing Tara sitting there with those two boys and the mother who only wanted her son to be a priest, Anne realized that looking back the pictures it was those three and then she remembers that Father Frances married them. Anne couldn't help but smile and wish that she would have the kind of friendship and love that they have for each other.

Mike smiles at Anne and says, "You need to know that whenever you hear Tara yell or just walk away, she can never leave those two. It's her place in this world to make sure that those two are taken care of.

Thomas has this gift of seeing what people need to know, Father Frances is the voice of God, and poor Tara has the job to make sure those two stay on their path."

Mike places his hand on Anne's hand and gives it a gentle squeeze.

Anne looks at him and then looks at the empty table and smiles.

Anne watches as Uncle Thomas and Father Frances walk back to the cottage.

CHAPTER 9

LATER THAT DAY THERE WAS talk around town that Devlin was buying a dressing table, dresser and a wardrobe. Why does a bachelor need a woman's dressing table and wardrobe? Many say that maybe Devlin is ready to settle down and start a family.

Uncle Thomas got wind of this on the way from the fishing trip with Father Frances. Uncle Thomas needed to get home to Tara to let her know about Devlin and this mystery woman. Thomas had to get home. He had to get to Tara. He wanted to keep Anne way from all the stories.

Thomas knew if Anne got wind of any of the rumors, she wouldn't even bother to pack, she would just leave.

Devlin finally bought the last piece of furniture for the bedroom. He smiled to himself. There were the pieces she picked out the last time they were at the store together. If only she was there so he could see her face. To see her jump up and down with joy. He remembers when she was happy they hugged and she'd say, "Bounce with me." Devlin smiles at the memory.

If only things worked out like they've planned. He would have been bouncing now.

Just then a song on the radio brought him to a particular night that they were at the pub. They weren't there together, they were just at the same place at the same time.

In fact he was sitting at the corner table watching her. It was a couple days after they met. Anne was having a great night with Thomas: laughing, singing and drinking.

He heard her say 'my gums are numb' as she orders another drink.

The local boys were playing some American music, mostly country, for Anne. She was dancing with Thomas in those cowboy boots that made Thomas that much smaller. She really shouldn't wear anything that make those legs longer than they already were. The boys started playing a song that Devlin recognized but couldn't remember the title. It was a famous country music song.

Anne yelled and grabbed this poor boy off the bar and started dancing with him. The music got louder and so did everyone in the bar.

The only thing Devlin noticed though was Anne: her smile and the way her eyes light up when she laughs.

Anne looked at Thomas who was at the pub sitting down waving her on to enjoy herself.

Just then the fiddler player started a soft melody and the pub was quiet. Everyone stopped what they were doing and just listened, even Anne, as she was to let the music take her to a magical place. As the song told its story. couples stood up and danced. Thomas took Anne's hand and they, too joined everyone in the softness of the song and the moment.

Anne closed her eyes and softly smiles as Thomas tells her the story of the song, the legend and laughs as he was probably telling a bunch of blarney.

Devlin found himself laughing too. He watches as Thomas kisses her check as he sits at the bar.

Anne looks up at Devlin and to his surprise she is right in front of him taking his hand.

Quietly he tells her, 'I don't dance.' But that didn't stop Anne. She took his arms and wrapped them around her waist. Looking into his eyes, she said, "Just feel". Stepping into his arms, Anne felt like she always belong there.

Devlin always thought he wouldn't ever settle down. He was just that kind of man. But having this woman in his arms, spinning her around and around, he was dancing.

Shaking his thoughts out of his head, trying to get that image out of his mind and the feeling he still had of Anne in his arms. Devlin needed to focus on the task at hand and pray to God that he can get through this without injuring himself. Looking at the pieces on his front lawn, wondering how in the hell he's going to get them in the house.

Just as Devlin approaches the wardrobe, a truck pulls in. Devlin walked around the wardrobe to see who it was. He sees Will, one of the teenagers from town who works part time at the grocery store during the summer. He climbs out of his truck and smiles, "Any idea how you're going to get these in all by yourself, or should I help?"

Devlin smiles, knowing this boy all his life, Will was always a helpful child and has turned into a helpful young man.

"Will you know no one likes a smart ass." Says Devlin as Will helps him lift the wardrobe into his house.

CHAPTER 10

ANNE WAS ON HER LAST frame looking over the pictures on her lap top.

There was something about this one picture she took of the town square that didn't look right. For some reason the picture she took of the now famous bench made her stomach sink. She rubbed her eyes, thinking to herself. Your just tried. You're looking for something that's not there.

Going through more photo's she stops at the picture of a field of flowers she took on one of her walks.

She didn't notice it until just now but the flowers looked like the ones she had in her hospital when she was giving birth to the kids. The picture brought her back to the room with the great big window that had a painting in the corner. The painting was a small picture of a little fairy and a flower looking up to the sky. Anne would focus on that picture when her contraction would start. She also looked at the two little outfits Aunt Tara made her. One was yellow and the other was green.

Uncle Thomas had made a beautiful wooden train and a jewelry box that played the most beautiful song she ever heard. Years later she found out Uncle Thomas wrote it. The nurses were wonderful. When she felt alone she looked at her two healthy, beautiful babies. The nurses were right there to her a tissue, an ice cream or just a hug. One of the nurses told her ice cream will make everything better.

Having her kids without Devlin wasn't her idea of a good time but her parents were great. There were times during her pregnancy that she wished Devlin there. She wished he was there when she found out she was having twins. She wished he was there when her son kicked her like she was his own personal kicking bag.

Their babies first picture, their daughter was hold her sons hand.

Anne had a terrible time when she had brought them home, laying them down in separate cribs was a mistake.

Those two would cry until you set them next to each other or until they were holding each other hands.

Anne would smile as she looked down at them in their crib. She would have a wave a loneliness that would grab her. The loneliness was replaced with anger as she thought about Delvin missing our baby's lives.

'Well it was his choice! Damn that man!'

How could one man bring back some many emotions good and bad?

She saved all the pictures and went to check her email. Going over the junk mail and deleting them.

She sees her mother emailed her. "Just checking in to make sure you're ok." Her mother wrote. "How is your visit?" Anne's mother always knew if anything wrong or if anything was going on with Anne.

Anne wrote her mother that she was fine and she should be done in a couple of weeks.

Anne asked about the kids and told her mother not to spoil them too much. Anne didn't tell her mother about running into Devlin. In Anne's mind if she doesn't bring him up her mother might think he moved or got married.

Then she will stop telling Anne that she should tell him about his kids.

After sending her last email to her editor Anne thought it would be a good time to see Mike. She needed a beer.

CHAPTER 11

ANNE WAS IN THE HALLWAY when she hear, Aunt Tara saying, "Are you serious? Why are people saying that? What reason do they have? Who is this girl?"

Uncle Thomas said, "I don't know but you know anyone who is near him will be tied to this rumor."

Anne stopped in her tracks thinking 'Who are they talking about.'

Aunt Tara laughs, "Just because he bought bedroom future."

"Tara, he bought the dressing table and the wardrobe."

Anne's heart stop, 'dressing table and wardrobe? No it can't be mine. It's been twelve years it can't be the same one. Those have been sold by now.'

Anne tries to shake the memory of that day she found the in her words, 'the dream set.'

She remembers Devlin laughing, when she told him to bounce with her. She can't remember the last time she bounced.

"God I'm pathetic.' Anne picked up her camera, as she headed towards the door, "I'm going to the shop."

Aunt Tara yells back, "Bring back me some great pictures."

Anne saying, "That's all I take." as the door shuts.

CHAPTER 12

DEVLIN PULLED INTO HIS DRIVEWAY and he smiles.

He can't wait to see Jamerson face when Devlin show him the new fishing pole. That little boy will jump out of his skin.

As Devlin takes the pole out he can't but think of that little boy and what he lost at such a young age.

Seeing Anne back in town did stir up old memories, it seems that her attitude towards him hasn't changed for the better.

Devlin talked to Thomas and Tara when Anne left.

They do keep him up to date on what Anne is doing.

The book deal, the calendar and the numerous awards she won for her pictures. The album he has of her, pictures she took of the two of them or the time he took the camera and focus it on her. Some were really good and the pictures of herself he downloaded on the computer and the articles are all in a photo album he has. Sometimes he thinks it's a little creepy if somcone picked it up, would shake that feeling off and think his just so proud of her and what she has done with her life.

He figured she would never see it so what's the harm.

Devlin took the fishing pole and placed it in the shed with the tackle box. As he sets it against the wall he notices, on the shelf a piece of paper. He picks it up and turns it over, he realizes it was a picture.

It was the picture he took of Anne. This picture he took with her camera the first day they met. Devlin remembers that day like it was yesterday.

Devlin looks out towards the tree. This tree was where he first laid eyes on Anne.

Devlin was in his work shed when something caught his eye. He waited and then he saw it. Why did his tree have feet? Someone is in the tree, 'Oh for the love of Pete.' he stormed out of the work shed,

"It's a damn tourist." This happens every once in a while. Someone takes a wrong turn but they usually end up at his door not in his tree.

As he reaches the tree he hears, "Oh for the love of Pete!" and he sees something falls from his tree.

The bare feet ascend from the tree, then the legs.

As the person, who's leg seemed to go on forever reach the ground, he noticed a fine rear end. As the young lady hit's the ground and goes on her hands and knees, "Oh come on how far could have you gone?"

Devlin smiles, as he watches her, she searched through the grass, and looks at her hands.

The way the sun high lights the red in her curly hair, Devlin wanted to get lost in the curls.

Devlin smiles and says, "Excuse me."

Anne jumps and turns to see this tall broad shoulder dark hair ice blues eyes man smiling at her.

Anne places her hand on her heart and says, "Oh my you scared my belly.'

Devlin tilts his head to see her beautiful face.

"Sorry that I scared your belly but my I ask what you're doing in my tree? Can I help you find whatever you are looking for?

Anne stood up reaching his chest in her height. Ann smiles, "Oh Thomas said that I could get great shots from this tree and I lost my bracelet."

"OH! there you are." Anne reaches across the ground towards, Devlin leg. Devlin watches as she reaches for the bracelet. He could smell her perfume.

Apples he smiles apples. Anne is on her knees as she places her cuff bracelet on her wrist.

Devlin knees down to her level, "So Thomas told you that my tree was the best spot for what?"

Anne looks up, "Yes, Thomas told me this tree would give me the best shot but he didn't say anything about you. Sorry, I didn't think that I was on anyone's property. I'll just climb back up to get my camera and shoes."

Devlin smiled, as he watches her climb back up

"Wait, your shoes?"

Anne smiles and looks back, "Yeah they're next to my camera." As she said that they fell out of the tree and nearly hit him on the head.

Anne laughs, "Oh I'm sorry I should had said look out below.'

Devlin smiles, Devlin believes that was the moment he knew he had just falling in love with Anne. That moment was it. To see her smile and laugh that's all it took. During that first day they talked, laugh sang.

One night as just the sun was going down, Devlin took the picture of her. The picture Devlin is holding Now. He smiled but then he started to feel the pain of the last day they were together. How could one picture hold so much happiness and yet so much pain. Devlin places the picture in his back pocket and slowly walks out the work shed and head to his house. Jamerson will be home from school and Devlin promised him that he was going to take him to the same spot that Devlin father took him to. Sarah was going to drop off Jamerson. It was going to be a boy's night out.

Devlin went back into the house and pack some sandwiches for their fishing trip.

CHAPTER 13

DOWN THE ROAD ANNE HEADS towards Betsy store to see Sammy. Anne smiles she couldn't wait to see her.

Anne reached the door Sammy reached it before

Anne could open it and jumps into Anne's arms.

Sammy screamed, "I can't believe you're here."

Anne smiles, "Yeah I'm here,' and Anne notice

Sammy was fat, "Sam your fat! Fat in a great way.

Oh Sweetie your knocked up."

Sammy laughs, "Oh my Love this is my third." As Anne and Sammy look at each other, they smile.

"So how is Paul?", says Anne as Sammy usher her to the table by the counter and Sammy sits across from Anne.

"Paul is fine he watches the kids during the day while I work and during time off from school. He works part time at the mill in the other county."

Anne smiles, "God Sammy you're a mom, I'm sorry to hear about your mom. She was a grand lady and I just loved her."

Sammy reached out for Anne hands and squeezed them and smiles. "She loved you like you were one of her own.

You were like a sister to me and when you left . . ." Anne looked down at her hands, "Sammy you know why I left. It just wasn't working out. I had nothing here that would make me want to stay. I do love you guys, I would have loved to stay here. I couldn't live in the same town that he lived in. To have all the looks from everyone had given me and Devlin. He was here first so it was only right that I would be the one to leave."

Sammy smiles, "Well that is just stupid, you left this town because a man."

Anne smiles, "You stop, you would had done the same thing if you were in a different town and you had no reason to stay.."

"You had a reason to stay and you had a reason to run, whatever was the reason you will tell me when you're ready, won't you Anne?"

Anne smiles, "It's scary how you can read me."

Sammy shook her head, "You have the gift too Anne. Mom told me and I see it too."

Anne smiles, "So how long will I have to wait before you offer me some of your mothers bread?"..

Sammy laughs, "I just made some it should be out of the oven just about now." They both stood and walk to the back of the store where the ovens are.

Ann quickly grabs a piece of candy on the way. As she was chewing, she says, "I don't know how you guys make this chocolate so good but I'll have to buy a pound of it."

Sammy smiles, "Sarah's little boy love the chocolate too."

Anne stops, "Sarah has a son?" Sammy turns, "Oh, yes. He is the kindest and sweetest little guy you would ever met. He just loves Devlin, those two are inseparable. You can find them together at the old pond where Devlin went with his father."

Sammy notice as she was taking the bread out of the oven that Anne was pale and looked a little shaken up.

"Anne are you ok?" Sammy asks her.

Anne looked up, she looked like she was hit, "What, Oh yes I'm fine. How long has Sarah and Devlin been together?"

Sammy smiles, "They're not, not that I'm aware of. Devlin does spend a lot for time at her house. Her son looks to Devlin as a second Dad. Anne I really don't think Devlin got over you."

Anne looks at Sammy with a shock look on her face, "Sammy it's been twelve years and our relationship is in the past. Devlin has moved on. Nobody would blame him if he moved on but Sarah, she was always a thorn in my side I don't know how she how he could be with her?"

Anne took a deep breath, "It doesn't matter Sammy, I came here to take pictures for my new book. To see the people I love and who love me."

Just then the front door open, with the sound to the bell.

Anne and Sammy looked at the counter.

There was a little boy who could be Devlin's son waiting alone for Sammy to wait on him. In his hand was the candy and money. Anne wasn't ready to meet him yet and Sammy could see that. Sammy smiles as she leaves the room.

Anne looked at her feet, wishing she was in any other place but here. Anne couldn't deal and slipped out the back door. 'Yes you are a coward but not now not that little boy.' Anne tells herself

CHAPTER **14**

TARA WAS IN THE TOWN square when she saw Anne walking from the back door of Sammy's shop. Tara notices that Anne was walking rather fast like she was escaping or running from something or someone. Then the answer to her question walked out of the shop, Jamerson happily skips out of the shop with his favorite candy and a loaf of bread.

Tara smiles, thinking to herself, 'That is one happy little boy.' Then it is like she was hit Tara stopped, 'Oh no. No, Anne you don't think. That little boy does have name the same as Devlin's father.'

"OH MY.", Tara had to get to Thomas this can't be true Devlin wouldn't, not her, not that girl.

'Why didn't I think of that first, that can be the reason.'

Later that afternoon Tara enter, their cottage to found Anne in the sitting room watching one of the movies she bought Tara from the States. Anne was lying on the couch. Tara could tell that Anne really wasn't watching, the musicals that Anne brought over per Tara's request. Tara thought this movie wasn't a good choice. When she sees that the part she walked in on was the song about love found and lost or something like that, just when the music ended Anne sat up with the remote and hit the mute button.

Tara sat down in her chair next to the couch.

Anne notices her as she stood up, "Oh Aunt Tara, I didn't know you came in."

Tara smiled, "I just came from the Town Square."

She waited for a reaction but Anne just smiles. "Oh did you get anything. I was there I could have picked it up for you."

Tara smiles, "Yes I know I saw you leave the Shop.

You looked like you were in a hurry. Where were you going in such a hurry?" Anne got up and walked to the window, taking a deep breathe, "OH Aunt Tara I just have to finish taking my pictures and leave."

Tara stood up and walked towards the window,

"Anne, what happen? Why do you feel you need to leave this place? This is and will always be home to you with people who love you."

Anne turns to Tara and winks, "I have to finish my work and leave. I can't stay here no matter how much I would love to. As you know I have reasonability's."

Tara smiles, "Don't you think you should let the person know about the reasonability's. After all he has a right to know."

Anne looks up, "Aunt Tara you know I can't. After the things he said. After all we burned that bridge."

Tara wanted to say more but she knows that look it just wouldn't get her anywhere. She let Anne walk out the door. Tara just hoped that the walk would give Anne some clarity. She hoped that Anne would at least think about what she has said maybe just maybe as Tara looks on.

Anne walks in the field that the outlook of Ireland would give Anne the idea that if he knew about her reasonability would change Anne's future and his.

CHAPTER 15

DEVLIN AND JAMERSON WERE WALKING up the lane when Jamerson point with his fishing pole, "D who is that?"

Devlin looked in the direction of the fishing pole was a lady a lady with red hair. Just at the moment Anne looked and saw both of them. Devlin could tell on the look on Anne's face that she was shock to see them.

Nowhere to run Anne took a deep breath and walked towards them. 'Don't blame the child he is the only innocent one in this situation.' Anne tells herself.

Devlin places his hand on the child's head and walked toward Anne.

Jamerson smiled as the two grow ups meet.

Anne smiled at Jamerson, kneeling down to his level, "Hello, sir." extending her hand.

Jamerson gave a shy smiled and takes Anne hand.

Anne smiled and Jamerson giggles, "Hello Anne."

Both Devlin and Anne were surprised that he knew her name.

Anne looked at Devlin, "Hello Devlin. How was your fishing trip?"

Devlin smiled, "Hello. Fine we didn't catch anything this time." He looked at happy little boy as he rubs Jamerson head. "There is always next time."

Jamerson looked at Anne as he held out his fishing pole, "Anne, did you see the new pole D got me!"

Anne noticed that Jamerson called Devlin to see the excitement on that little boy's face, Anne really didn't react or ask. Why Jamerson calls his father D?

Anne smiles, "Wow Jamerson," as she inspects the pole very carefully. Devlin smiles, he was happy to see that Anne still had her way with children no matter how she thought or felt about him. It was nice she didn't behave rude with Jamerson.

Devlin watched Anne very carefully as she looks at his new pole.

Anne looked from the pole to Jamerson, she tilted her head, "Why Jamerson," looking at the wide eyed little boy and smiles as she hands back the pole. "You are a very lucky little boy." As she looks up at Devlin, "This pole if you take care of it, will give you a great number of fish and wonderful stories to be share."

Jamerson looks at the pole in his hand and looks up at Devlin and smiles. "Did you hear that?"

Devlin smiles, "Well Jamerson I heard some poles are like that but I didn't know if this one was a lucky one."

Jamerson smiles. "Wait until I tell Ma!"

Jamerson took off running, Devlin laughs, "Hey Little man you be careful!"

Anne watches as Jamerson runs, Anne turns to Devlin, "Aren't you going with him?"

Devlin looks at her "No he's fine. His mother is watching out of us just up the lane."

Anne felt her heart drop, thinking to herself his mother, your wife a child you share with that woman.

Devlin looks at Anne, "You ok?"

Anne smiles, "Yes, I think I've been walking to much today."

Anne knew it was a lame excuse but it looked like Devlin bought it.

"OK, you do look like you have been doing too much.'

Anne smiles thinking of Devlin concern. "But you have always done things yourself."

Anne couldn't disagree with him with that because it was true.

"Well I should be getting back. I have to send my pictures to my editor."

Devlin nods, "Well I better get going I have to get home I have some cleaning up have to do."

Anne looked at him, "good bye."

As she turns to walk away Devlin takes her hand,

Anne looks at him questionably, "Have a good day O'Hara." he squeezed her hand in his. Anne heart still reacts to his touch. He let go of her hand and walked away. It happened so fast Anne didn't have enough time to react or yell at him for calling her O'Hara again. All Anne could do is watch him walk away.

Anne walks back to the heart of the town. She needed to talk to someone, 'But who, not many people know why I left.'

As she tries to figure out how she was going to deal with her heart over riding her brain.

Going through the conversation she just had with Devlin. Reminds her of a conversation they had so many years ago. Anne was just asking Devlin about his family because she hadn't seen any pictures. She never heard him talk about his past.

One of the few pictures he had in his place was one of himself and his best friend Matt. Devlin told her that Matt was one crazy son of bitch. A grand friend even though he was a Brit. Devlin said with a smile on his face. Anne smiled but still she knew nothing about his family. Devlin looked at her like maybe she should drop the subject. There was so many times that she did but she had to, after all she was in love with this man and he was her husband.

"Anne, I really don't have much to say about them. Can we just drop it?."

"Devlin why? I am your wife and if we are going to have children don't you think they might want to know their grandparents from Ireland?"

Devlin looked at her with a questionable look.

"Children?!? Anne I don't want children, I don't want to bring kids into this world with everything out there. The times are just getting tough with kids know a days. I can only imagine what it will be like when they get older."

Anne smiles and says, "Devlin every generation has said that and if that was true I doubt we would had gotten this far in our generation."

Devlin was shaking his head, "Look Anne, don't you think I will ever change my mind don't think of trapping me into having children. I've seen women far too many times try to trap men staying with them by getting pregnant. I will not stand for it and", at this time he as pointing his finger at her with such angry and rage, "if you think of ever doing that I will take you and that thing to the airport so fast you won't know what happen."

Anne stood in shock. How could this man stand in front of her be the same man she falls in love with? Anne couldn't stop the words as they came out of her mouth, "You Bastard! If you think I would ever want to bring a child into this world with you and are sadly mistaken!"

Just, then she finds herself in front of the Candy and Bread Shop. Still feeling the pain and anger from that argument was the first step back to the states. She sees Sammy outside the shop smiling over her cup of coffee.

To Anne it seemed like Sammy was waiting for her.

Anne smiled and walked towards the shop as Sammy opened the. Anne quietly sat down at the table in the corner as Sammy closed the door, Sammy then locked the door and turned the open sign to close.

Sammy sat down across from Anne and slid a plate of bread in front of her. Anne thought to herself it's so good to have friends that supply you with great bread.

"So Anne, do you want to talk to about it now?'

Anne looks up from the untouched bread, "Oh Sammy it's just everything. How can I trust my heart when my head is yelling at me to run and don't look back.

Sammy smiles, "Anne why does your head yell louder than your heart?"

Anne knows that she needs to tell Sammy her story.

Ann looked up and smiles as a single tear fell from her eye. Sammy reached across the table and squeezed Anne's hand.

Sammy smiled, "Love you need only tell me what you can, don't tell me everything just what you can."

"Sammy I need to tell you everything. I need your help."

Anne took a deep breath, "Ok, I'll start from where I thought I made the biggest mistake of my life. You see, I thought I found the man of my dreams. Everything about our romance was like out of a dream, I wasn't looking for a husband, I met Devlin I thought.. but boy was I wrong." shaking her head.

"After we got married, I was, what I thought building a future."

Sammy smiled, "So how old are the twins?"

Anne without thinking, "They will be eleven."

"Sean is his father and Elizabeth is more me . . ."

Anne all of a sudden covered her month, "Oh GOD!"

Sammy reached for Anne hand and smiled, "Anne you don't need to hide your secret is safe with me. You really need to tell their father. How do the twins deal with no father, what did you tell them?"

Anne touched the unity pendant around her neck.

"I've told them that their father and I lived in two different worlds. That we really didn't know each other." Anne took a deep breath and continued,

"Lizzy would like to visit Ireland but Sean is so much like his father he would rather stay. Sean sees no reason to travel and would like to go some place warm." Anne smiles, "He is so stubborn."

Sammy smiles, "You should have brought them.

Can you imagine Tara and Thomas reaction? Those kids will be their grandchild's in their eyes."

Anne smiles, "They know about the kids, and the kids know about them too. You should have seen the Christmas gifts they sent last year."

"Oh Anne, you really should tell Devlin, he has the right to know. Anne their father."

Anne nods, "Why do you think I'm in this state Sammy. To see him with Jamerson, I just can't. I was wrong not telling Devlin but when I found out I wasn't in the right state of mind. I was hurt, angry and I wanted him to feel the same way I felt."

Just before Anne finished her story there was a knock on the store door. Both girls looked and there was the man.

Devlin cupped his eyes so he could see why the store was closed. As he looked in the store, their eyes might. Devlin felt a pain the pit of his stomach.

Why is Anne in the store with Sammy and it's closed?

Why does it looks like Anne is in pain and why does this feel like?! I need to get to Anne! Devlin then started to pound on the door, "Hey Girls let me in!"

Sammy winked at Anne as she got up to open the door. Anne felt like she was going to faint.

Maybe this was the right time to tell Devlin about their kids.

Devlin couldn't get into the store and reach Anne fast enough. When Sammy open the door Anne stood up she wasn't sure why but she had the urge to run and run fast.

Devlin was at Anne's side like he had wings.

"How are tricks O'Hara?" with that smile that still made Anne toes curl.

Anne shook her head, "You really know how to talk to a girl."

Devlin smiled, "Well I never had a complaint."

Anne took a deep breath, 'Yeah that's true.'

Anne looked down on the table then looked at Sammy, straightening out her back, pulled her shoulders back and said, "I need a drink" and walked pass Devlin and Sammy and walked out.

Devlin raised his eye brows and said to Sammy,

"What was that all about? Is Anne ok? Why were you two in here what is wrong with her?"

Sammy looked at Devlin, "You two really need to talk."

"Why do you think that?"

"It isn't my place Dev."

"But if she is in pain or hurt or.." A painful look went across his face. "Is Anne sick?!"

"Devlin, you just need to talk. You two need to just sit and talk."

Sammy walked past him and up the stair as fast as her pregnant self would take her.

Devlin was at a lost what is going on?

Well he isn't going to just stand here like a fool.

Anne has secret then she can keep them, 'Why should I care. She walked out on me not the other way around. Damn I need a drink too.'

Devlin left the shop with a heavy steps and a slam of the door.

CHAPTER 16

DEVLIN FOUND HIMSELF AT THE cottage. He thought this would be a good time to get back to work. The contract from the gentleman in the New York branch want a sketch of the of the office building that had the feel of on old Irish building. The New York branch wants their whole community to have the feel of Ireland. As he enters he could almost except to see Anne on the couch with her legs out stretch, her nose in a book and the scent of apples and coffee.

Anne always had an apple candle burning and a cup of coffee. She would be in another world with a book rubbing her feet together.

Totally unaware that Devlin walked in watching her.

Devlin had enough of the memories of Anne.

Maybe it was time to get her back and find out what really happened to them all those years ago.

Devlin walked to his desk on it was the start of his work. As he sat he goes through the piles of papers and finds a picture. The sketch he did of Anne.

She was holding a baby. Devlin couldn't remember the little one name. The look that Anne had in her eyes as the baby smiled up at her and they locked eyes made Devlin heart hurt.

At that point in time he could never see himself a father. The thought of it scared him feel scared to death. He knew right there and then she wanted to be a mother.

How can one remark say out of angry end the most important relationship he ever had. Devlin couldn't even remember what the argument was about or why they were having a fight. Devlin didn't mean what he said, only she just stayed just one more day. He knows that they would be together, maybe with a couple of kids of their own. He turns in his chair he could see his son running down the stairs with a teddy bear in his hand joining his little sister who is in his mother arms. How can that scene feel so real be so right. Devlin knows that it was only a dream unless he can get Anne to talk to him and find out what happened to them, to their love.

He stands in takes a deep breath and heads toward the liquid cabinet. Taking a shot of whiskey Devlin turns and heads back to his desk. He sits grabbing a pencil, "Ok Dev, you have to finish this and then you will get your family you were told you would have."

Devlin smiles, 'You were told.'

'How can Aunt Tara know that? How can she sound so sure? Did she know something I don't or maybe it was that sight that we people have. All but you Dev, your too stubborn to believe in the sigh.'

Devlin smiles and started with his work. The passion he felt for Anne. The love that they had be together is used to finish his project for the New York branch.

CHAPTER 17

ANNE FINDS HERSELF ON HER second drink and wonders what the kids are doing. She looks at clock on the wall across from her and as she looks up she sees herself in the mirror. She was pale and her eyes, she is tried. She needs to finish and get the Hell out of here.

Just then she hears. "Well, well, looks who's here."

Anne closes her eyes and takes a deep breath.

Sarah sits next to her. Mike looks and walks over from the other end of the bar.

"Now girls, I really think that we can just have a quite night, right?"

"Michael love, I was just sitting here waiting for my third drink please."

"Anne, I hope you're waiting for someone."

Anne turns to look at her, "Uncle Thomas is running late." and waves Mike with another drink.

Mike slowly walks over the replace one empty pint for a full one.

Sarah smiles, "Mike I'll have the same.'

Mike nodded his head

Sarah looks at Anne profile "Anne"

That tone coming from Sarah voice made Anne sit up and look at her. Anne couldn't decide if the tone was a 'I'm sorry for acting like a high-schooler.' Or 'I feel sorry for you because of Devlin.'

"Yes, Sarah."

"Anne listen I know that I've haven't been the."

"Sarah just say it. You and I have been acting like two high school girls in love with the same boy."

Sarah smiles, "I was going to say a bitch but I like your example better.'

"Sarah I like yours too.'

Anne looks up, "So you want to tell me why you are sitting here?"

Sarah looks at the empty glass, and she starts to play with it.

"Have you ever thought you wanted something so much then you realize what you wanted wasn't yours to begin with? It wasn't what you really needed."

Anne looks at Sarah and smiles. "I've been known to make a few mistakes for time to time, but why did your decision cause you to hate me

The statement made Sarah squirm in her bar stool.

"Anne, I never hated you. I just hated how easily he fell in love for you. When I was looking for it and needed it so bad."

Anne looked surprised from that statement, "Easy! You have no idea how much I went through before I got to Ireland, I wasn't looking for love it found me." Anne waved for more beers to Mike he nodded and poured the drinks.

"Sarah I went through so many types of men in the states. I date one for 8 years. We dated broke up and dated. I was the one person he would ask for advice. He took me car shopping to help him decide on the best car. His clothing, Hell I even help him pick out his house."

Saran laughs, "You're kidding?"

Anne took a drink, "No I am not. At the end of our relationship I just told him I couldn't' have him in my life when I am looking for someone to marry I wanted someone to have a family with and I knew he wasn't the right person for me."

Sarah was suspired by that statement. "God Anne I don't know if I could have done that. I stayed with that person because I didn't know if I could be alone."

"Sarah I would rather be alone than in a relationship with a person who doesn't love me. It's the worse feeling knowing that you deserve better and your letting that person use you."

Mike hears that and thinks to himself, 'Damn that girl, Anne just smile and watch your sharp tongue and just shake hands.'

Then the sound of Sarah laughing and then Anne made him smile and breathe a sigh of relief. He had a mess to clean up from those two.

Just then Uncle Thomas sits down. "I see you two have finally realize that you have more in common than you think.'

Anne stops and looks at Uncle Thomas, "What do we have in common, Uncle Thomas.'

Sarah looked at him to with a questionable look on her face.

Mike walk to Thomas and handed him his drink.

Thomas drank the dark beer and continue. "Well ladies you have lost your faith in love."

Anne rolled her eyes and Sarah laugh.

Sarah stood up. She finished her drink and places money on the bar. "When there is talk about lost love that is time for me to leave. Mike." Sarah point to the money she placed on the bar, "This is for this round."

Anne smiles, "Sarah have a good night."

Sarah nods, "You too Anne."

CHAPTER 18

UNCLE THOMAS TAPPED ANNE'S PINT with his, Anne looks at him.

"Yes, my dear, you want to explain about the statement." Anne says.

Uncle Thomas smiles, "I really couldn't say. It's something that you have to find out for yourself. You wouldn't believe me if I told you."

Anne took another drink. "You and your blarney."

Mike nods, "How about some coffee Dear."

Anne looks at her pint glass, "Yes I believe I Would like some coffee."

Uncle Thomas, "Now that's a smart one.

Have a clear head and you will make the right choice. Stop listening to your head, listen to your heart."

Anne stands, not waiting for the coffee, "On that note, I think I'll go."

Uncle Thomas turns as he says, "Why, are you so stubborn?"

Mike laughs, "Oh Thomas herself can handle this, we gave her our advice. Let her make her own mind."

Anne walks back to the bar, she leans over and gives Mike a kiss on the check, "Thanks Mike.'Mikes blushes.

Anne winks and walks out of the bar. Anne looks up at the sky and takes a deep breathe. Not knowing where she is going to go but somewhere that will help. She wants to pack her bags and leave but there is something holding her here. 'It can't be a man.'

She will not put her life on hold especially when her children are involved. 'That's it that is why she can't leave, because their father.'

"Damn, that man.!" Anne yells.

Anne walks back to Aunt Tara and Uncle Thomas cottage. The cottage was dark and empty. Aunt Tara was over a friend's house and Anne left Uncle Thomas at the pub. Anne was rather happy that she's alone. Anne walks into the kitchen and takes a beer out of the fridge. She walks to the living room.

It's a large room, large enough to dance. Anne walks to the radio and puts in her favorite mixed cd. The song started slowly, Anne sat in the chair. The song became very familiar too familiar. She placed her hand on her heart as she listens, she started to cry. It wasn't the song that was just tear her heart apart was. It was the feelings, that was engulfing her. Anne stood up to turn it off.

She couldn't, all she could do was listen as the memories of her and Delvin flash in her head.

The laughter the smiles and the tears. All the plans they made and finally the promise that broke them apart.

Anne sat back down as the tears kept coming. The song ended. Anne took another drink of her beer.

Suddenly she realizes that one of the kids put her music together.

She smiles, they knew. Her children knew that their mother would be here with their father. Anne took a bigger sip of her beer. She stands, "Damn those kids.

Why do they have to be some much like their father?"

Another songs comes on, she walks to the cd player and she turns the volume up. 'Ok, kids bring it on!'

Getting herself ready for the next song,

Anne shakes her head as she sat down, the tears fall and with a smile she leaded back in the chair and closes her eyes.

CHAPTER 19

DEVLIN IS DEALING WITH HIS own memories. He walks through town not really thinking about the direction. He finds himself at Thomas and Tara's cottage. He hears music. He walks around to the back to get a better view from the window that looks into the living room. The music he hears is country. He would know that song anywhere. Anne use to play it when every she was in her 'Black Irish mood.'. The mood that meant she was sad and sometimes she didn't know why. The song would help her get out of the mood.

Devlin was a fan too but there was another song that he would listen to. It would help him and remind him of herself. He gets to the window, there she is dancing with her eyes closed and a Guinness in her hand. He smiles thinking, 'God she is beautiful.'

The songs end's and then softly he hears two voices coming from the cd player." Mom." She stops and looks at the cd player, shocked. "We remember you use to play this song. Maybe it will bring back your smile. We love you and remember Mom, No sad."

Anne smiles, she used to say that to the kids when they were babies crying when she trying to get them to sleep. Then the song starts.

Anne takes a deep breath looks down at her empty beer bottle and walks back to the kitchen.

Outside Devlin really couldn't hear what was said just the soft sound of a voice. He couldn't tell what the message said to Anne that made her smile. Smile like she use to when she would look at him. He looks down at his feet, 'damn I miss her'

Devlin walks to the front door. he hears ending to hear "Not coming down till sun comes up."

He knocks on the door, but Anne turns up the music and she can't hear Devlin knocking. He lets himself in. As he walks through the cottage he hears her singing and watches her dancing to the music, he reaches the arch way to the living room he sees Anne dancing and her back was towards him. He smiles and says to himself, 'Damn she can move.'

Anne turns and yells, "Oh Shit!". She realizes she wasn't alone. The one person is this whole wide world that she couldn't deal is standing right in front of her and that person with one look, one small smile could and still do make her heart stop.

Devlin smiles, "Sorry O'Hara I didn't mean to scare you." Anne walks to the cd player but Devlin was right behind her. He reaches for her arm, "Anne please leave the music on. I haven't heard that song in a while. You know I still have that song on tape we use to listen too."

Anne takes her finger off the stop button and looks at his hands on her arm. Looking up at him she said in a quiet voice, "Why are you here?"

Devlin smiles, and pulls her into his arms and says looking into her eyes, "Because you need me." With that he pulls closer, lifts her chin up and kisses her. Anne sighs as the kiss becomes deeper. Devlin pulls her closer to him as her hands move from his chest to his shoulders.

The kiss opened the flood gates of pent up emotions from both of them. The hunger. The fear that if they stop. If they don't, then the song comes on.

Anne freezes. Devlin feels a wall, the wall builds up is Anne.

As he looks into her eyes he sees the fear, the sadness of the death of their past, their marriage. Devlin softly wipes the tears from her check.

"Oh my Lady why, why the tears?", Anne pulled her face away from his hands. She can't tell him she can't say what is in her heart. "Why are you here? Why now?"

Devlin felt her pull away from him. Then he hears the song. He looks at her, she sees that he feels the same way as she does. Devlin turns away from the her, turns his back to her. Devlin feels his eyes well up with tears. How can one song fill a room with so much emotion that could tares two people in a passionate embrace apart.

Anne asked again, "Why, why are you here?"

Devlin walks over to the cd player to hit the stop button but he turns the volume up. Anne jumped and Devlin quickly turns it down. He looks at her saying, "Sorry."

Anne sits down in the arm chair, rubbing her forehand, as Devlin sits on the coach. He looks across the room to he, Anne.

"You ask why I am here."

Anne looks up at him, tilts her head, "Yes I did."

Devlin smiles, "I was walking through town when I realized I was here. I don't know why I ended up here." Anne looks at him with a look that told him she wasn't happy with his explanation. Devlin shook his head. Understanding that his explanation really didn't tell Anne why but it was the truth.

"Anne I don't know what else to tell you. That is the truth. I can see that you don't like the reason but there it is."

Anne took the bottle of beer and finished the last of it. Devlin smiles, "Do you want another one? I'll grab us one more?" Anne nods her head as she hands him the empty bottle of beer. As he walks into the kitchen, he hears her say, "Yes I would like another one, but you must leave. I can't have you here. I just."

Devlin looks into the living room from the kitchen as he sees her rubbing her head. He knows by the way she is rubbing her head that she should go to bed. Devlin shuts the refrigerator door empty handed. Anne looks up to see Devlin walking towards her empty handed.

"Ah, did you forget something?'

Devlin stops in front of her and bends over, before Ann can say anything? Devlin picks her up.

Anne was shocked and mad, "What the hell do you think you are doing? Put me down right now!" Devlin smiles and walks her down the hall not saying a word. Anne kicking and yelling, "Damn it Dev put me down." Then she realizes that Devlin was carrying her to the bedroom.

"Devlin you really need to put me done. Just what do you think you are doing?"

Devlin approaches the bed and sets her down gentle and he sits next to her.

Anne sits up she is shocked to find out where they are.

"Devlin, why are you here?" her voice cracks.

Devlin takes her hand and kisses it. "Good night O'Hara."

And with that Devlin stand ups and leaves. Leaving Anne with more question and no answers.

CHAPTER *20*

AS ANNE CRIES IN HER bed, Devlin walks home with the sounds of a quiet song and the sound of Anne asking, 'Why did you come here?' as Devlin walked to his cottage. He tried to think of an answer to the question. The answer is just as simple as 'you needed me'. Devlin shook his head and continued walking with mixed emotions. He felt wonderful for just a fleeting moment Anne was in his arms, his O'Hara was back. The woman who still has his heart no matter how hard she tries to denies it. He knows she still feels something for him too.

After walking for hours Devlin made it back to the Cottage. He enters the cottage and see's something in the rose bushes under the large picture window.

He kneels down for a closer look to his surprise it's Gary.

It was a rope necklace that had a monkey or troll holding a heart that he bought Anne. She was so excited when she saw it during a music festival.

He smiles, remembering the day she called in tears telling him she lost Gary. At first Devlin didn't know who she was talking about then it came to him, 'Oh that crazy looking necklace he bought her that everyone talked about.' She was heartbroken when Gary never turned up. Now it's like a sign. It's like Gary knew he was needed.

Smiling to himself he walks in the cottage with Gary in hand looking for a safe place for Gary.

Devlin will know where he is and use Gary when he is needed.

The next morning Aunt Tara told Anne that they were going on a little road trip. Anne was still tired from last night and really didn't want to go anywhere.

She just wanted to go through her pictures, check her email and talk to the kids.

Aunt Tara and Uncle Thomas ambushed Anne in the kitchen with the idea.

Accepting the cup of coffee from Aunt Tara. Anne sat down, Anne couldn't say no to Aunt Tara and she knows it.

Anne takes a cup of coffee to the kitchen sink and turns, "Ok you guys, what do you have plan for me?"

Aunt Tara smiles, "Well there is this shop in Athrown. You can you can take your pictures, you remember it's by the sea."

Anne remembers, a wonderful little town but there was something going on, she knows if she asks, she wouldn't get a straight answer. 'Just go with it Anne', "Ok you two I'll be ready in a half an hour."

Tara looked at Thomas and smiles, "Are you sure he will be there?" Tara asked looking down the hall making sure Anne doesn't hear.

Thomas smiles, "Ah me dear he will be there and he has no idea that she will be there too. We need those two together. I just hope.." as he stands up to get another cup of coffee. "that we aren't making a mistake. You know that those two can be the most stubborn people."

"We can at least see that they both need each other and they can't live without each other."

Tara signs, "I know they need this and they will be together only she would tell him."

Thomas shook his head, "Only herself knows why.

I just hope she tells him soon because it's been long enough having those kids not knowing their father." Tara smiles, "Oh please you want those kids here with you." Thomas smiles as he walks out the door to his rose garden, "Damn right where they belong here in their home country."

Aunt Tara pulls in to a parking space in front of a in her words, 'A cute little shop.'

Anne gets out of the car she falls to her knees and pretends to kiss the ground.

Tara walks around the car to witness what Anne was doing. She shakes her head, "Oh you, I don't drive that bad."

Anne stands with a shocked like on her face, "You saw that truck, right?"

Tara smiles as she walks towards that cute little store,

"You are over reacting."

Anne says, "You are one cool dame Tara."

Tara turns, "You have known idea my girl."

After the first hours of pink, too cute and lace, Anne really needs to get out of the shops.

Maybe a large plate of French fries or walking down the road to more pictures for the book.

Trying to remember if there was a pub on this street or the next.

Tara turns to ask Anne if Elizabeth would like this.

She can see Anne had enough, "OK my dear I'll see you at the pub."

Anne was packing her pocket book and getting the packages together that she bought the kids. Aunt Tara says without looking up at her,

"Remember we still have one more stop before we go home."

Anne looks at Aunt Tara, 'She is up to something.' but right now she needs to leave this shop with pick flower dresses that she will never see her daughter in.

After she put the packages in the trunk of the car she heads down the right side of the street and turns left, 'Now, what side feels right?' Anne thinks to herself.

Then she sees it, the rainbow, "Ok, you win."

Anne takes her camera out from the back seat and heads to the right a little excited.

This isn't the first time her question was answered with a rainbow. It had something to do with her in a tree and a pair of blue eyes.

Around 2 Anne enters O'Malley's restaurant the lunch crowd was pretty over. There was just a hand full of couples and a group of men in a corner.

Anne smiles at the bartender as she sits down. The bartenders greets her with smile and says

"What can I get you my dear?" Ann looks at the menu, "I'll take a diet soda, and I'm waiting for one more person so just a soda right now."

In the far corner of the restaurant were two men.

One of the men is Devlin and a man with blonde hair almost the same built as himself but a few inches shorter. They were going over the pictures and ideas, Devlin brought with him to help the New Yorker. Their museum and housing projects for the look of Ireland without leaving New York.

This private contractor and business man came to Devlin with their ideas and wanted him to run with it.

Devlin still has no idea how they found him or how they knew that Devlin could do this sort of thing. Devlin pulled out the last of the project plan, "Like I said over the phone, will this lay out it will show all the details of the stone work and the yellow roses will get direct sun light."

Douglas the head of the project, looks up at Devlin,

"Devlin why yellow roses. I've notice that all the gardens have yellow roses. Not red, pink or purple but yellow and they are Irish yellow. Any reason for this." Devlin looks at him and smiles, "Well let's just say that we all have our own little secrets. Ok"

Douglas just smiles, "Ok, ok I understand. It's a lady or mom, I get it"

Devlin was going to tell Douglas were to go then he hears "If I should fall from Grace with God", on the radio and smiles.

Douglas looks up from the paper work to ask what's with the smile he hears the song.

"Do you want to dance?"

Devlin smiles, "Sorry, you won't let me lead. I rather have another round."

Douglas turns towards the bartender and lifts up his empty glass.

The bartender smiles, "Excuse me my Dear, but this party is high tippers."

Anne smiles, and then she hears a familiar laugh her heart sinks. 'That's Devlin, I know that laugh." Anne stands up and places money on the bar ready to leave when Aunt Tara enters.

Anne see her reaction when Tara see's Devlin at the Table. At the point Anne knows that she was planned to be here with Devlin. 'I can't believe she is still trying to do this. Why, she knows.'

Tara smiles and then she sees that Anne knows who is here and knows Tara knew. Tara says, "Ok Ok you know so what do you want to do. Do you want to eat or leave?"

Anne smiles, "You knew he was here, why are you doing this? What do you think will happen? Things are so far gone that it can't be fixed. You need to accept this and move on. Now on that note. I don't want to leave because I'm hunger as long as he doesn't see us I'll be happy."

As girls sit on the other side of the bar, to make sure Devlin can't see them.

After a nice lunch, Devlin didn't notice them, but Anne noticed him as he left with his party of well dress gentleman. It made Anne happy knowing that she help Devlin build dream.

His drawing was unbelievable. His plans to build up the cottages that were left before they disappear around Ireland. His image would final come true if Anne to say about it. With his talent and her connections with that gentleman who left with him.

If Devlin knew she was responsible for this meeting.

The reason that Douglas knew everything about Devlin, his talent, his dictation and his love of Ireland. He would never accept anything from Douglas corporation. Devlin would probably never forgive her but what choice did she had.

An opportunity she had for him never forgetting the last time they were in the same room, the fight, those words that can never be forgotten or taken back.

If Devlin know about the work she had to do to get Douglas firm to even look at his work she found on her PC. her or that she dated Douglas after their marriage.

The thought of all of that coming to light made Anne's get a cold chill.

CHAPTER 21

ANNE DECIDED TO DRIVE BACK to the cabin. Aunt Tara was fine with it. It was nice to have a fun day shopping with Anne. As they pull in the driveway Anne notices that the front door was open, music from her cd player was on and two fishing poles lean up against the cottage.

"Oh Lord, if those two have those dirty things in my kitchen I'm going to kill them."

As they reach the front door they hear, "Mike did you see the size of it."

"That I did my friend. Where did we leave the bottle? Who sings this music?", as Brad Paisley sings, "Then".

"Its herself music, it was in the machine, it's better that other stuff the kids call music."

As the girls enters the kitchen there they are. Two grown men who should had known better, but there they are. Happy with the trophies on the kitchen table. A whiskey bottle almost empty. Country music playing on the cd player. Aunt Tara surveyed the display the two were making. With her hands on her hips Tara says, "Thomas David and Michael Frances, this time you two have done it. How many times have I've told you? I don't want those ugly things in my kitchen!"

Uncle Thomas smiles, "Oh Me Darling you should had seen it."

Father Frances stands with his hands out stretch in front of him, "Oh yes Tara Darling it was one hell of a fight." and falls to his sit.

Anne smiles thinking 'oh boys you are in trouble, big trouble this time.'

Aunt Tara isn't smiling. She shakes her head and says, "Enough!"

Both men stopped. Aunt Tara tuned off the music.

There was such a silence in that room it scared even the Lord himself.

After Aunt Tara told the boys that they aren't to see each other for two weeks, " The only time is at mass

There will be no free time for the both of you.

Do you understand?"

As Uncle Thomas and Father Frances cleaned up the kitchen Aunt Tara smiles at Anne as she leaves the boys to their mess.

"I don't like yelling at them like that. But when those two get together there is no way of telling what kind of trouble they can get themselves in to."

Anne took the packages into her room and started to take the items out to the bags. She knows she bought too much already but this was Ireland who knows when the next time she will be back.

She notices her lap top on the night stand The light was flashing letting her know that she had an email.

She looked at her watch it she thought it was too early for anyone from the States to be emailing her.

Anne reach over to get the computer. Placing it on her lap as she sits on the bed. The email is from Douglas, she read it with a smiled. Douglas wrote

"The project is going great. He is so sick of yellow roses I really would like to tell Devlin who is responsible for his great fortune."

Anne felt her heart stopped, and says,

"Yellow roses, my favorite flower."

Anne replied to Douglas email, 'you can't tell him, not yet. Just keep this for me. I'll tell him, if I have to. I don't see any reason why. I won't be here in Ireland much longer. Then I will out of his life and he will be out of mine. Thank you for everything.'

Anne felt better. What was Devlin doing with all the yellow roses?

Anne got up off the bed and placed the lap top back on the night stand, telling herself, "I can't think about this, I have to get my life back."

With that she grabs her camera bag and headed out the door.

"Hold it right there my dear, you have a package."

Anne stops to see the package Aunt Tara was holding.

Anne smiles and takes the package from her.

She places it on the kitchen table. Anne sees from the address it's from the states, her mother.

"Oh yes!" Anne exclaim with excitement.

Even before she opens the package,

Uncle Thomas walks in to the kitchen and stops.

"Oh Lord we aren't going to have that God awful meat thing in our house?"

Anne smiles as she opens the package and pulls out three tin can's for Potted ham. "Oh YES!! Love you mom!" Anne does her little dance while holding the can's in her hand above her head as she dances around the kitchen table and stops in front of Uncle Thomas, "Yes this will be in the kitchen and it will be eaten in your kitchen and.." Stopped dancing and walked into the hall way, "Eaten in the hall way and I don't say anything about your black and white pudding." as Anne make a face that says she didn't like. "It at least I tried it and you won't try even my sandwich meat!" Anne stuck her tongue out dancing back into the kitchen seeing Aunt Tara laughing. She places the package on the counter off the kitchen table. "Ok, you two enough.

Anne where do you want the items to go?"

Anne stops to look into the package pulling out mayo, Twizzlers, and a large bottle of hair junk.

As Anne calls her hair jell that helps her hair have some control in the Ireland weather.

"Anne your Mother has packed everything but that candy we like." Uncle Thomas said as he looks in the package. Behind him Anne holds up the two large candy bars. For Aunt Tara to see and smile.

With a wink Anne's packs the item's back into her box and leaves the candy bars on the kitchen table for Uncle Thomas to see. He laughs as he notices and grabbing one and heads to the living room.

Aunt Tara yells, "If you eat the whole thing in one sitting

I will not share mine when you still want Anne's chocolates"

Anne leaves her bedroom after she places the box in her room.

Aunt Tara saw Anne leave with her camera, she winks, 'Why can't you just tell him you still love him.'

THAT NIGHT DEVLIN JUST FINISHED his work on the last idea Douglas had about the walk way between the store and the houses.

Devlin had to admit that it was a better lay out then he had. Maybe Douglas does have an eye for Ireland. Devlin always thought it was a little weird that Douglas had a great picture of Ireland when this was his first trip. Sometimes when he talked to Douglas it seemed that Douglas knew Devlin more than just a man he hired to do a job. It was like Douglas had a list on everything Devlin.

Devlin takes the sheets of his work off the table and placing them in the carrying case. Devlin rubbed his neck and walked to the couch. As he sits down with a heavy sign,

"Now if I can only get pass this. I could get a good night sleep." Looking across to the fireplace on the mantel was their clock. A beautiful clock they received from Uncle Thomas and Aunt Tara on their wedding day. Aunt Tara said it belonged in her family for generations. The clock stopped working on the day Anne left. It was a weird to have time stop. It didn't help that she was back and yet the clock still didn't work. Devlin smiles as he looks next to the clock and there was Gary that crazy little monkey just smiling back on Devlin. It was like Gary was mocking him.

CHAPTER 23

MAYBE SHE WILL GET LUCKY this morning since she didn't get any good pictures yesterday.

Anne was walking down a lane that just screamed the history. The beauty and the heart of Ireland. As she reaches the part in the road, she could take the right would bring her back to town and the left would take her to her past. The cottage she shared with Devlin the cottage where her heart was broken.

Maybe is still here. She didn't think she could handle seeing the place just yet.

'So if I just walk just close enough to take a picture, to show the kids, to see where their parents once lived'

When she reached the tree, that reminds her that just over the hill was what once her home. She took a deep breath and continued walking. There it was. The sun shined on it like it was telling her that her cottage was there. A quiet building that holds so many memories, laughter, tears and fights.

Anne smiles, as she remembers about the fights and the make ups. She wonders who's living there now.

What kind of people they are? Are they happy? Do they have kids or is it an older couple?

She remembers talking about growing old together.

Anne hoped for a rose garden in the back and a wonderful chair swing to watch their grandchildren play in the back yard.

As she reached the gate to the cottage Anne felt her heart stop, 'You've gone too far, your too close.'

Anne pushed the gate open not going any closer she just took one step and at that point she reached for her camera. Taking pictures of every angle of the cottage. As she reached the back yard. There it was.

Anne stopped like she hit a wall. Her heart stopped.

All she could so was just place her hand on her heart. A beautiful rose garden and a chair swing.

'I knew it would look great. Well at least I know I sold it to the right people.'

Anne didn't take pictures of the garden or the chair swing. She thought to herself that it wasn't necessary. 'Besides I should get out of here, the people of Ireland are great but I just can't see who lives here.' Knowing that the cottage is being taking care of is great but to see the people who live in it would be too much. Anne quietly walked back to the front of the cottage. She didn't want to look inside as she passed the windows. Anne made sure she couldn't see, she kept looking forward. She closed the gate. Smiling she pulls her I-pod Touch. Placing the ear buds in her ear she hit's music button and started to walk. The music started loudly, it was Van Halen, "When it's love." Anne stopped, 'Dam that boy.' Her son Sean is in to her music. Anne smiles she can remember hearing this album on his computer and him yelling to his mom,

"Hey mom hear this oldie. Isn't it great."

Anne reached the tree and not looking back she just took a deep breathe, 'I will never go this way again.'

Later that day Anne arrived back to the pub, 'I need something to eat.' she enter to see Thomas and Father Frances at the bar talking to Michael. They look back, and smiled, "Hello Darling." Uncle Thomas says, "Been taken a walk?"

Michael smiles, "What would you have Darling?"

As Anne reaches the table near the bar where she places her camera down. She gives each of them a hug. Stepping up to the bar and leaning over the bar to give Michael and hug. Anne says, "Mike, I could go for a fat sandwich."

Michael smiles, with a tear in his eye and gives her another hug, "Oh have I have missed you." he whispers in her ear. Michael was so happy to have that wonderful girl back in his pub. He knew when she felt her Irish in her it was time for a sandwich.

With that he goes to the kitchen with a bounce in his step.

Anne turns to see Father Frances and Uncle Thomas looking at her with a goofy smile on their faces.

"Ok, you too you aren't supposed to be playing together."

Uncle Thomas smiles, "Well you see my dear, after we told herself that if we can just meet at Michaels, and Michael promises to watch over us and will report back to herself."

"So you see my dear Thomas has it all set."

Father Frances smiles with such a look on his face.

"You know my dear Michael will only make those, sandwiches for only you.", Father told Anne as he walks behind the bar to get a diet soda for herself.

"Thank you, Father Frank." reaching for the glass.

"He is the only one that can make that sandwich,

I've tried to make it for kids but I just couldn't get it right."

Thomas smiles, "Frances, did I show you're the new pictures of themselves?" as he reached in his pocket for the couple of pictures of the kids that Anne took before she left for Ireland. Father Frances sits back down between Anne and himself. Uncle Thomas smiles, as he brags about Sean's grades and the talent of talk for Elizabeth. As Anne listens she notices that Uncle Thomas sounds like a proud grandfather. The times he and Aunt Tara missed with the kids. Anne can't think that way it will only make her sad. She decides to call the kids. In her jeans pocket she looks at the time. The kids should be home. She dials, and it only took one ring,

"HEY MOM".

That was how Elizabeth answers the phone just like myself, Anne smiles, "Hello Me Darling."

Elizabeth laughs "Mom you have the talk."

Anne, "I know my sweetie, it's hard not to have the talk when you are with your Grandfather Thomas all the time."

"Mom's with Grandfather Thomas!" Elizabeth yells over the phone.

"Mom, can we talk to him?" Sean gets on the other phone.

"Of course my dears."

The men look up from the pictures but Anne walks back to the bar, "you have a phone call Uncle Thomas."

Thomas looks at her questionably, "Hello?" and then a tear and a laugh, "Hello My Loves, yes, yes." he walks to the back of the room to get some privacy.

Father Frances smiles and reaches for her hand to see Anne crying too.

"It's just not fair. Frank. Those three love each other so much it just breaks my heart."

Just then Father Frances says, "You need to tell himself."

Anne smiles, squeezes his hand. She looks across the bar to see Michael, in hand with a fat sandwich and a smile. Setting the plate down in front of them.

Anne looks at the plate. That has the most beautiful sandwich "No way." Anne looks up at Michael, who has the biggest smile on his face. "Michael Patrick, I do love you." Uncle Thomas sat at the bar with Anne's phone in hand, "You remember extra potatoes fries."

Uncle Thomas slid the phone to her and steals a fry,

"Himself takes pride in his potatoes, and you are the only one he fries them for."

Anne grabs half the sandwich and bites into it.

"That's right!" with a month full of food and smile.

CHAPTER 24

AFTER A GREAT MEAL AND a couple of beers Anne was heading back. She notices that she had a shadow.

Anne knew who it was without looking. Devlin was behind her but why? 'Why not just ask him what he wants.' With that little statement to herself, Anne stops and turns to face him.

Devlin was a little surprised that she just stopped and was waiting for him.

Anne decides to end this, waiting for him to reach her. As he got closer, her heart beat was beating faster and faster as he reach's her.

"Ok Devlin what are you doing. Why are you following me?

Devlin was going to lie but it's time.

"O'Hara, I saw you leave the pub and I know that smile. So did you share any of the fries?"

Anne smiles, "It's funny that you know me so well."

Devlin smiles as Anne turns and walks away,

"O'Hara you haven't answer my question."

Reaching her, Anne laughs, "Your right Dev, I didn't and you know why. You know the answer. I never share my fries with anyone."

Devlin laughs, "You remember that time the plate of potatoes Michael made for you. You finished that plate. It was like you never had potatoes in your life." Devlin smiles. Anne smiles. It was a good day and a great plate of potatoes. Anne remembers that the potatoes became the only food she ever craving when she was pregnant with the twins. It was too bad Anne never found out what Michael put in his spuds.

Just then the clouds roll in and with a clap of thunder the rain felling from the sky. Anne jumped, "Holy Crap!" Anne's shirt was becoming transparent and her jeans were becoming her second skin. 'Oh Great, just what I need. Where can I find a place to hide?'

Devlin couldn't help but notice what the rain was doing, and the effect it was having on him. 'Damn! why can't we.. Don't do this Devlin, you need to just take it slow. No matter how great she looks in wet clothes.' He smiles as he notices that Anne was getting embarrassed.

Anne see's him smiling, "Oh wipe that smile off your face."

Devlin smiles, "Sorry O'Hara it's just I've seen you in must less than a wet t-shirt. I have to admit it's nice to see that the girls have gotten better."

Anne was covering her top with her arm across her chest. Hitting him with her free arm, "You need stop enjoying yourself, Dev." Anne says.

The rain continues to fall down. The thunder was moving across the county side.

They were walking as they reached the fork in the road, then thunder clap was right above them.

The noise was so loud causing Anne to jump. Anne notice that the rain is getting harder.

Devlin grabbed her hand and ran, "Come on O'Hara. The storm is getting too close."

Anne notice that they are running towards their cottage, 'Why is he, what is he doing?' Anne wonders.

As they reach the gate to the cottage. Anne stops dead in her tracks. Devlin turns to see, "O'Hara why are you stopping. We have to go in it's raining really bad and the lightening."

Anne looks from the cottage to him, "Why am I stopping? We can't just go in there. I don't own it anymore." As Devlin pulls her closer to the cottage.

"Remember!" Anne says.

Devlin says with a grin on his face, "Oh O'Hara I don't think the owner will mind if we go in and get dried off."

Devlin pulled Anne towards him. She was in front of him and at the front door. "Anne just open the door."

Anne turned to look at him.

With a questionable look on her face. Anne opened the door and there she saw it.

Their past, their furniture.

Devlin had a smile on his face. "O'Hara," he still had her hand. He pulled her closer to him, "I bought cottage from you. I couldn't have anyone else live here."

Anne looked at him with such angry. She couldn't understand. "What, why."

Anne just couldn't understand she was shocked.

'Why had Devlin bought our cottage? Why didn't Aunt Tara tell me? What's his game?'

"You bought my cottage? You bought my bedroom set, the swing and roses?" Anne was on the brink of tears as the joy Devlin felt turned panic.

"Anne." he tried to reach for her, but she pulled away.

"No! NO!" She didn't want to hear anything more from Devlin, she needed to get away, and fast.

"Anne, just listen, you need to know why I did all this."

Anne can't get past this. She needed to think.

"Anne", she finally heard the plead in Devlin voice.

"No, No Dev. I need time, I can't think."

Devlin pulled her towards him, into his embraces.

Anne tried to pull away but he had such a hold on her. She just wanted to stay in his arms but, "You bought the cottage." The tears started to fall and she couldn't stop.

With anger, she pulled away from him, she looked down at her feet. Wiping the tears from her face. She looked up at him with a look that made Devlin step back.

"This is why I never told you about the kids. You do this." as she turns to see the living room of the Cottage. "Your games, it was always about you!"

With the sound of Devlin's in take breath made Anne realized what she said.

"Oh God!" she covered her mouth with her hand.

This wasn't the way she wanted to tell Devlin about the kids. As she looked at him she could tell that he was shocked. The look was like he thought she said kids but he wasn't sure. She walked pass him. Away from the cottage back to town. He didn't realize how long he was standing at the door way of the cottage until he saw that she was all ready passed the tree. "What the Hell!"

Devlin was fast at her heels. The rain was still coming down hard but neither one of them could feel it. When Devlin reached Anne he stepped in front of her. Taken her hand to stop her. He knew she was still crying. "Anne stop."

She can't deal with this now. She needed to talk to Aunt Tara. She needed to find out. Why he bought their cottage. Why didn't Aunt Tara tell Anne?

"Anne, look at me." she took a deep breath. As their eyes meet, Devlin smiled, "Kids?!?".

Anne smiled, "Sean Patrick O'Rourke and Elizabeth Sarah O'Rourke."

Devlin smiled and with a tear in his eye, "I have a son and a daughter." Anne nodded, "Your son is just like you the most stubborn twelve year old, I ever met."

At that point Devlin realized that he doesn't know his children.

Then it sank in. She kept his children away from him. "You never told me, you kept my kids from me for 12 years." Anne became just As angry as himself, she yells, "I kept them from you!??!?, Oh no you!" throwing her arms in the air.

"This was all you. You can't handle even the thought of kids. You couldn't talk about your family."

At that point she was pointing at him. "It was all about YOU! We weren't married we were just."

Anne had to stop she know that she shouldn't say anymore. She had to stop before she would say something she might regret.

Anne knew this day would come. She didn't think it would be in the middle of the road in Ireland with the rain pouring down on them.

Anne looked at Devlin. She could read his face. The joy was very readable on his face. He was happy about the kids but anger was fast growing a crossed his face.

Anne took a deep breath. She did so badly wants to take his hand but she still was upset about the cottage. Their kids and the secret was more important than the cottage

Maybe if he can just listen for the kids' sake they can be friends at least for the happiness for their children.

"Look Devlin, we had that fight I was back in America. We just signed off on the cottage. The divorce papers were in the works when I found out I was pregnant. All I could see was that look on your face when you told me that it was a mistake, our marriage. We should have never gotten married let alone met. Whenever I bought up kids or you parents, well you know the rest."

"How could I ever go back to you with 'oh by the way I'm pregnant.'. I didn't want you to stay for the only reason was because of the kids." Anne started crying again.

Delvin couldn't stop to wonder was the reason for the tears are for the kids or herself. Devlin didn't know what to say all he knew was he needed time.

"Look, I know this isn't the time or place to talk about this." That's was when they but realized that they were wet. Devlin took her hand, "Come on, let's get you back to Aunt Tara's and Uncle Thomas. I need time to take all this in."

As they reach the door to Aunt Tara's gate the rain was slowing down to a drizzle. "You need to get inside and get dried off, I'll talk to you later." Without good bye Devlin turned around and leaves her standing there wet, a little relieved and confusion.

CHAPTER 25

THE NEXT MORNING FINDS ANNE at the kitchen table looking at her coffee cup. She didn't get any sleep. All she could see when she closed her eyes was the look on Devlin's face. She really needed to figure out what to do. She would like to just pack her bags and leave but that wouldn't be fair to the kids. She realizes they need to have their father in their life even if it's 12 years later. Taking a sip of coffee that's realizing that there is no coffee in her cup.

Aunt Tara enters, taking the coffee cup out of Anne's hand. She pours Anne a cup and take a cup for herself.

Tara sits down across from Anne and places the cup of coffee. Taking a sip of her coffee Tara says,

"So tell me my love, did you give it any thought on just how you tell Devlin about the kids. Was it just that thought of someone else in your cottage with your husband?"

Leave it to Aunt Tara to get to the heart of the problem. Anne looked up from her coffee cup, "Well you know the mood just felt right. I thought what the hell why not tell him."

As Anne stood up and pours the coffee in the sink. Just then Uncle Thomas come into the kitchen. He had a smile on his face but when he sensed the tension in the room he walks to the sink and gently took the coffee cup from Anne's hand.

"Me Darling I'll take that cup before it's becomes air born."

Anne didn't realize that she was shaking with the cup in her hand. Aunt Tara got up and take her hands. "Look love, I know you were upset and hurt. You never wanted to let Devlin know about the kids that way but you did. Now you have to finish this."

Anne pulled away from Aunt Tara. Walking back to the table and sat down.

"I know but Devlin needs to take this all in. I will give him time. I also need to take this all in too. Why didn't you guys tell me he bought the cottage?

Did you know what he has done with it. The whole place is just like how we wanted it to be. With the yellow roses, the swing in the back yard and the furniture. Did you know about the furniture?

It's just not right I don't want any other woman in my house,"

Aunt Tara smiles, "What makes you think there's another woman in that house but you?"

Anne looks at the two of them, "Look you two. I know you guys want us back together but it's not going to work. I have my life back in the states and Devlin has his here. I wouldn't want him to be guilty into a relationship with me. We will talk when he is ready. We will do the right thing for the kids. That's the most important thing. That will be the only relationship we will have after what we have put each other through.

CHAPTER 26

DEVLIN WAS STILL SITTING ON the couch looking at the fireplace. He's been there since he got back from walking Anne to Aunt Tara and Uncle Thomas house. He has have twins, "I have a son and daughter."

Devlin was happy and mad. 'How could Anne keep this secret from me? How could Aunt Tara and Uncle Thomas not tell me?

Then he wonders, how was her pregnancy? Was it hard? What did she look like? He missed out on feeling her stomach. Hearing the babies heart beats, their births. If only he could had taken back those words. You can't change the past. All you can do is learn and try not to make the same mistake.'

Devlin looked at the fireplace mantle and saw Gary smiling at him. "Well my old friend we have twins, a boy and a girl. She named my son after my grand da, and my daughter had my ma's name too." A tear was forming in his eye, he wiped his eyes and smiled, "I wish I wasn't still in love with that woman." He stood up and headed out the door.

CHAPTER 27

TWO DAY LATER ANNE WAS in her room trying to figure out how she's going to have a conversation with Devlin. She needed to think of a way to start this. The phone ringing jumps her out.

Aunt Tara enters Anne's door, Anne thought for sure her heart was going beat right out of her chest. She turned to see Aunt Tara smiling at her.

"You don't have to worry my dear it's Sammy she is in labor. She needs you. Paul is going to take her to the hospital. She wants you to watch the kids."

Anne felt relieved. She has to 'watch the kid?'

Aunt Tara smiled and hands the phone to her.

With a wink Aunt Tara leaves, Anne smiles, "Hello, Hey girl. Yes I'll be right over. Will the kids be ok with me?"

Three hours later Anne is on the floor between Sammy's two kids. Betsy her oldest is 4 and Peter just turned 3, are watching another movie on Anne's lap top. The popcorn was almost gone. Anne quietly got up while the kids were deep in the movie Anne was thankful that the kids were big fans of American cartoon movie.

Paul called about an hour ago. Sammy was in full labor and it's going to be any minute. Poor Paul he sounded like this was his first time being in the labor room.

As Anne started to make more popcorn she remembering when she was in labor with the twins.

She missed having the whole experience of having their father there. She tried to reason with herself that it was the best for both of them. At the time Devlin wasn't part of their lives.

Remembering the look on Devlin face, the hurt, the angry and the lost.

Microwave beep alerting Anne that the popcorn was done.

Suddenly Anne realizing she made the wrong decision.

It was only for her feelings.

To make things right for herself, Devlin and their children.

As she goes back into the living room she finds Peter fast asleep and Betsy fighting her heavy eye.

Anne smiles, placing the popcorn on the coffee table she kneels down next to Betsy and whispers in her ear, "Come Sweetie, you need to get to bed."

Betsy looks up at Anne and smiles sleepy, "Did the baby come yet?"

Anne shakes her head. As she helps Betsy gets to her feet, "Not yet Betsy girl. When you wake up tomorrow morning, you will have baby to help mommy and daddy to take care." Betsy turns to look back at Anne, she smiles saying as she enters her bedroom, "I'll be the grandest older sister there even."

Just as Anne kneels down to pick up Peter there's a knock at the door. Anne gently lifts Peter in her arm and walks to the door. She opened the door to be face to face with Devlin. Her intake breath made Peter stir. Anne rub his back, "Shh Sweetie it's ok." she whispers.

She step back to let Devlin, he enter. He says under his breath, "I knew you would be a grandmother."

Anne turns to look at him with a smile. Devlin looked up. 'she heard me.' Devlin smiled back as he sat on the couch.

Ten minutes later he sees her softly closing the kid's bedroom door. Anne walk towards Delvin.

Devlin looked away. He notices her lap top on the floor. She sat down next to him and places the lap top on his lap. He looks at her. Anne smiles,

"The kids were watching a movie's before they crashed."

Devlin looked a back at the screen and smile, "I smell popcorn."

Anne looks at him with a questionable look, "Yeah I made it for them while they the movies."

Devlin nods as he places the lap top on the end table.

He takes a deep breathe. Anne wonders what to say next if anything. just wait to see what he has to say.

Anne lean back into the couch with her arms crossed. Devlin lean forward with his hands on his knees. He took a deep breath and stood up. Anne watched him get up and walked to the opposite side of the room.

He looks at the pictures on the wall of a happy family. Finally he spoke which felt like hours but it was just a few minutes.

"Why couldn't this wall of a family be on our wall Anne?"

Anne hears his voice creak. She looks at her feet, her heart sinks. She knew she hurts him so bad that he didn't use his nickname for her, "Dev, we weren't in the right place. I was hurt and mad. We were getting

92

a divorce. Things were said I'm sure that we wish we could take back but we can't. I know that if I could I would have told you. I just couldn't get passed . . ."

Anne stood up and walked to the picture window that has a great view of the sea. Devlin was right behind her. He could tell she was crying. He places his hands on her shoulder. He gently turns Anne so they are facing each other. "Anne, I'm sorry that I said those words that I told you but my children?"

Anne nods, "I'm so sorry that you have missed twelve years. You can have the rest of your life to get to know your children and have them know you."

Devlin ask quietly, "Do you have any picture?"

Anne walks to her pocket book. Pulling out a small album. She motions for him to sit down on the couch, next to her.

Devlin nods, "Show me my babies."

Anne smiles, she opens the album. The first picture he sees are they twins on the floor. They both had Winnie the Pooh bears in their arms and where smiling.

Anne points to the babies in the picture, "This is Sean Patrick and Elizabeth Sarah. They were about nine months."

She hands the album to Devlin and leaves him with the pictures.

Anne finishes the last of the dishes when she hears Devlin clears his throat. Anne turns, "I hope we are better than yesterday." As she turns to place the dish rag neatly on the counter, Devlin sits down at the kitchen table with the album in his hand. He looks up at her and motions for her to sit down.

Anne takes a deep breath and sits down.

Her heart is beating so fast. It was taking everything she had to sit with Devlin acting like she was calm and cool.

Devlin takes her hand in his, "O'Hara."

Anne looks up at him. "They were the cutest babies.", and continue to say looking at Anne, "Why did I ever let you go?"

Devlin stands up and pulled Anne in to his arms.

Kisses her like this was need. Having her in his arms is like his next breath.

Anne sign and deepen her kiss. Devlin pulled her closer. Anne's hands moved up his chest and across his back. Anne wasn't sure how much more she could take without falling deeper and deeper.

The next thing she knows Devlin is pulling her down on the kitchen floor. His kisses went down her neck. His lips were working is way down toward her chest. He was unbuttoning her shirt and she was pulling his shirt off. It was like a tug of war fight between her shirt and his. 'This is crazy.' Anne thought to herself. Anne starts to giggle. Devlin looks up at her with a surprise look on his face.

"O'Hara, you weren't this sensitive before."

Anne smiles as she brushes the hair from her face.

"I just laughing because of this tug of war with our shirts."

Devlin smiles, "Kiss me.", Anne kisses him.

He had to admit she can kiss. As the kiss became deeper Devlin was able to get their clothes off. The kissing stop so they could look into each other's eyes. With a wink, in a smooth motion Devlin and Anne once again were one.

Anne couldn't help the tears. She thought to herself, 'I'm still in love with you.'

Devlin grabbed her leg, lifting it up.

Anne cries, "Oh, God Dev.."

As the rhythm was growing, Anne was reaching the point.

"O'Hara, you feel so good." faster and faster until,

Devlin let out a gasp and Anne, "OH OH OH!"

Devlin rolled on the floor with Anne in his arms so she was now on top.

Anne smiles, "You can't, NOW?!?"

Devlin winked, "O'Hara, I am too old."

Anne smiles and hit his chest, "Dev, you still have it. I can't believe it." as she looks around, "in the kitchen. It's not even my kitchen."

Devlin pulls her closer in a big hug, "O'Hara it wouldn't matter where it happen. It was going to happen sooner or later. Let me tell you I'm glad it was sooner because I couldn't keep my hands off you."

Anne's head was on his chest, she signs. She didn't want to think about tomorrow. She just wanted to enjoy this time together with him.

CHAPTER 28

IT HAD TO BE AROUND nine thirty at night. They were on the couch wrapped up in a blanket Anne's head. on Devlin's chest. She looks up at him and smiles.

Devlin looks down, and look at her questionably, "What's with the smile?"

Anne sits up and says, "I know Jamerson isn't your son but there has been talk. What happen to his dad?"

Devlin smiles, "Well O'Hara, Sarah was seeing this man from the UK. He was killed. She was going to move to his part of the world. After the car accident Sarah was devastates. With no family here or his family I just step up to help her."

Anne smiles, "You are a great friend and a wonderful role model." and squeeze his hand.

Devlin looks at her hand and continues.

"O'Hara, it' s not my place to say any more."

Anne smiles, "It's fine. You're a good friend."

Just then there was a knock at the door.

"Who could that be?" Anne stands up and walks to the door. Devlin is right behind her. Anne opens the door. To Anne's surprise she was face to face with Douglas. Without her thinking she says,

"Douglas what are you doing here?"

To Devlin surprise Anne knows the man who hired him

'How does Anne know him? Oh No, she set me up.' wonders Devlin.

Devlin quickly stands up. His movement made Anne turns around to see Devlin reaction. With the look in his eyes. She knows that he knows.

Douglas felt bad but was relieved at the same time.

Finally it was out. With the look on Devlin's face this was going to be bad.

Anne let Douglas in and turns toward Devlin.

"Ok, look Devlin, I told Douglas about your work. What you are capable of doing for his project, that's all. I didn't set you up."

She tried to reach for him but he step back.

Douglas figure, he should set things straighten.

"Look Devlin Anne told me about you, like I told her, just because we are dating I can't hire anyone my girlfriend thinks is good."

Devlin shocked looked went from Douglas to Anne.

'Oh crap.'

Anne shook her head and said, "Oh Doug, you should have said that."

Devlin lunged for Douglas. Douglas tried to move out the way but found himself up against the door.

"YOU Son of a Bitch!"

Devlin had Douglas pinned against the door.

All Devlin wanted was to hit this man so hard. How dare he think of his Anne in that way let alone say it. "Did you touch her?!"

Anne tries to pull Devlin away from Douglas.

"Devlin you're going to wake up the kids." Anne Says, Douglas looked at Anne, yes he was a little worried. Anne was pulling on Devlin's arm.

Douglas turn to look at Anne. Anne turns looks at Devlin with such pain in his eyes.

She knew this was bad. Not only did she hold back the knowledge of his children, she was dating Douglas.

Douglas the man who is responsible for his career.

Does he know his kids? All Devlin wanted to do was leave. "I have to get out of here!" yells Devlin

Anne tried to grab his arm. Devlin just shook his head.

Anne knew he needed time to figure this out. Time to understand.

CHAPTER 29

AFTER GETTING WORD FROM PETER that Betsy is great.

They have another little boy and all is well.

Douglas hugged Anne and told her he was sorry that he had shown up this way. Douglas thought Devlin needed to know what Anne have done for him.

"He isn't grateful now but he will be as soon as he gets over his busied ego."

Douglas said as they sat on the couch.

CHAPTER *30*

A FEW DAYS LATER ANNE finds herself sitting on Tara's couch looking at the blank television. It wouldn't be pathetic but she didn't notice or care.

The phone was ringing but Anne didn't notice it until it seems to go louder. That jolted Anne off the couch. She ran to get the phone and nearly knocked over the stand. "Damn!" Her foot hit the stand that the phone was on. Grabbing the phone, "Hello..?!?"

"Anne?"

"Yes, Michael it's me, how can I help you?"

Leaning on the wall holding the phone with one hand and rubbing her foot with the other.

"Anne, I need a favor?"

Michael sounds funny. Like he was scare or nervous, "Michael what's wrong?' the tone in Michaels voice made Anne stand up straight.

Anne becomes nervous.

"Anne is Aunt Tara or Uncle Thomas home?"

Anne walked in the window to see if their car is in the drive way. "Sorry Michael, they aren't home. Is there anything I can do?"

Mike sighed, "No sorry love you got enough on your plate. I'll check the pub to see if they're there." and hangs up. Before Anne could responds to his statement. "But of course he knows." Anne says to herself. Devlin has been gone for five days. Not many people know the full story just bit and pieces.

Anne was in just as unhappy as Devlin. So it didn't take a rocket scientist to figure that out, what was going on with those two.

Anne hung up the phone and went back to the couch.

Realizing that the tv wasn't on.

While she was reaching for the remote she hears a car door close. Aunt Tara is talking to herself.

"What an idiot! What was he thinking?"

Those statements made Anne place the remote down and reach for the door just when Aunt Tara open it.

Aunt Tara nearly walked into Anne, "Oh" she said with her hand on her heart. "Anne you scared me.

What were you doing at the door dear?'

"I heard you talking to yourself. Is everything alright?"

Tara smiles pats Anne hand and walked into the kitchen to place her bag of milk, bread and eggs away. Anne was right behind, watching Tara put the groceries away. Anne thought it would be a good idea to make coffee. Tara smiles and sat down waiting for the coffee.

Anne places a cup in front of Tara with a cup of sugar, a bottle of Bailey and Whiskey.

Tara looks up at the choices. Anne smiles, as she sat down across from her with her cup and the pot of coffee.

A couple of cups later Anne told Tara that if Michael needed help at the pub Anne would watch the bar but NOT cook! Tara smiles patting her hand.

"Oh Darling I know you can cook you just choose not to." Anne smile, "You Do understand!"

The girls start laughing and hug.

Michael kept asking Anne if she was sure she wanted to. Anne thought it was cute but then it got insulting. Anne yelled at him and told him if he asked her one more time she was just going to smack him. Michael had shown Anne where the liquor was. Once again he started to show her how to draw a beer but with a gentle shove Anne show him in her words, 'This is the correct way.'

After a couple of hours of the walk through. Anne told Michael, "Mike you're only going to be gone for a few days. You will be here tonight with me and I have Steve here too. I won't be alone." Michael says,

"I know love I just want you to be comfortable here.

Try not to have too much fun."

CHAPTER 31

ANNE HUGGED MIKE. HER FIRST night at the pub without Mike right there. Anne was a little nervous but she didn't let Mike know. Mike needed to deal with his issues not worry about the pub.

One night Anne was by herself at the bar. Steve went to the store to get more bread. They ran out way too quick, Anne didn't make Mike's fat sandwich, she made her father's chicken dish called chicken surprise. The dish could be with rice, bread, biscuits or mash potatoes. Her kids loved the dish. It looks likes the people here at the pub.

A lot of people were enjoying her dish thanks to Thomas who said he wanted the dish. He told Steve to cover the bar so Anne could make him his favorite dish from America. When everyone heard that they wanted it too.

As the days went by Anne was grateful for the distraction, helping out at the pub was a blessing in disguise.

Anne could get out of bed without effort and have a genuine smile on her face.

Anne knew she had to give Devlin time but was time a friend or was it the thing that tare them apart.

The pub started to play country music. At first it was just a quite song here or there for Anne. As the boys and some of the ladies of the town started to listen and loving it more, the louder it got.

When Devlin came down the stairs, he was able to slip in without being notice. Well that's what he thought.

Even with her back facing him, Anne knows he was watching her again and Anne couldn't read what his intentions are, just then Douglas walks in.

Douglas approaches Devlin and Anne is right there to stop if anything should come up.

Douglas looked Devlin straight in the eyes and said, "She wasn't mine to begin with."

Devlin looked at Douglas and slowing brought him down. Devlin nodded at Douglas. Anne got between the two men and look into Devlin eyes.

"We went on two dates, nothing happened. Dev, look at me." Devlin looked from Douglas to Anne.

"Nothing happened." Anne pulled on Devlin arm, he looks at Anne. She lets his arm go. Devlin went back to his table and sat down. He looks at Douglas and then Anne.

"Is there anything else I need to know?"

Anne looked at him then to Douglas, just then Douglas smiles, and turns to Anne.

"Well," Douglas reached into his pocket and pulled out a piece of paper. "I have a letter from Elizabeth to father." Anne looked at Douglas with a shocked look on her face. "Lizzie wrote Devlin a letter?"

Devlin wasn't sure if he heard Douglas right, 'Did Douglas just said he had a letter for me from my daughter?'

Douglas smiles and walks over to the table where Devlin was sitting. Douglas hands Devlin the letter. with a wink Douglas leaves.

Devlin sits staring at the letter. Anne thinks he is looking at the letter like it is going to blow up. Like it's not really in his hand.

Devlin looks at her, "Can you open it?"

Anne looks, as Devlin hands her the letter.

Anne carefully opens the letter and hands it back to him. Devlin took a deep breathe telling himself that he 'you can do this.'

Anne places her hand on his leg, "I'll leave with the letter. I think I am needed at the bar." She stands up.

Devlin grabs her hand.

"O'Hara please don't go. I don't know if I can read this without you here."

Anne nods and sits down next to him.

Devlin opens the letter, it reads.

I'm not sure how to start this, so let me just start off with Hello, I'm your daughter, Elizabeth Anne. Myself and my twin brother Sean Patrick just turned 12. I hope you and mom have stopped fighting. I hope you both are sitting down reading this letter.

We want to make sure you're not mad at mom. She doesn't know what we know. We know that you and mom had a really big fight. We've been told Sean is like you, all I have to say is . . . "Mom you are a saint."

Please know that mom isn't happy. I don't think she will ever be until you two knock this off and get back together. We know that you bought mom's cottage. We know that mom still has a picture of you."

Know this we don't blame mom. She had to do what she thought was best. You should know she is the best mom ever. We know you will be the best Dad. We are happy and healthy kids. If it's ok we would like to meet you.

Devlin had tears in his eyes, Anne carefully takes the letter for him hand and folded the letter and hand it back to him. She took his hand and squeezed. Devlin smiles pulling her in his arms and giving her such a hug. Anne just melted in his arms. "We are very lucky to have smart kids."

Anne laughs, "Sometimes too smart."

Devlin laughs, "So where are the kids now?"

"They are with my parents."

CHAPTER 32

ANNE AND DEVLIN WALKED HAND and hand towards town.

Anne looks at up at Devlin and he has a weird look on his face.

"Dev, what's the matter?"

He looks at her, "It's nothing."

Anne stops, "You know you can't lie to me."

Devlin says, "Do you think the kids will like me?"

Anne goes into his arms, "They will love you.

Sean might be a little stand offish but that's just how he is. Just give them time to get to know You and we will be fine."

Devlin hugs her. They head to Aunt Tara's and Uncle Thomas cottage.

Anne wasn't sure how the kids were going to understand that they live in United States and their father lives in Ireland. Maybe just maybe they can spend the summer in Ireland and for their Christmas break. Is that fair to everyone involve?

Anne couldn't stop thinking of all the fun they would have living here but would that be fair.

The people they would meet here and new family members.

The chance to discover Ireland for their selves.

As they get closer they hear loud music coming from the cottage. Devlin looks at Anne who has the biggest smile on her face. What they hear is music from her CD. The one kid's burn for her. The song is Van Helen, "When it's love."

Anne breaks free from Devlin hand and runs towards the cottage, "They are here!"

Devlin runs after her, "Whose here?"

Anne stops at the front door and turns to Devlin,

"Our babies."

The front door opens and there they are standing right in front of Devlin.

Devlin looks surprised. He looks at Anne then back to the kids.

Elizabeth stepped forward to Devlin. Devlin kneels down to the kid's level. They are small compare to his tall frame but tall for their age.

Elizabeth jumps into his father's arms, "Daddy!"

Anne covers her mouth with her hand. Tears starts to fall. She sees Aunt Tara and Uncle Thomas in tears with a huge smile's on their faces.

Devlin had tears fall from his eyes. All he could do what hold Elizabeth. He whispers, "Mo croi."

Anne know some Gaelic He said to her, "My Heart." A few minutes pass Devlin gentle placed Elizabeth down and looks at Sean. Devlin couldn't believe how much he looked like himself. Sean had the same look in his eyes.

Devlin thought to himself, 'he is yours son.'

Devlin walked over to Sean and held out his hand.

Looking straight into Sean eyes and saying, "Hello Sean I'm Devlin, your father."

Sean looks at Devlin's hand and slowly reaches for Devlin it. Devlin and Sean smiles as they shake hands. Then a surprise to everyone but Elizabeth Sean jumps into Devlin arms.

Now everyone was crying. The happiness, the tears, the laughter filled the cottage. From this point on their family was whole.

Aunt Tara and Uncle Thomas let the family have their time together. Tara had this look on her face that Thomas knew so well.

Thomas turns to her and says, "Oh no Darling are you sure?"

Tara smiles, "I only see one more but who knows what next year brings. As you know they said they wanted a large family."

Devlin and Anne have four more kids.

They had the great love story ever told in this small town in Ireland. Their love story will be told for generations to come.

Printed in the United States
By Bookmasters